THE FEAR COLLECTORS

LAUREN E. MITCHELL

SHOOTING STAR

SHOOTING STAR PRESS

First published in Australia in 2019
by Shooting Star Press
PO Box 6813, Charnwood ACT 2615
info@shootingstar.pub
www.shootingstar.pub

ABN 63 158 506 524

A catalogue record for this book is available from the National
Library of Australia.

MITCHELL, Lauren E.
    The Fear Collectors
    ISBN: 978-1-925821-19-2   PRINT
    ISBN: 978-1-925821-20-8   EBOOK

Edited by Katie Taylor
Typesetting by Debbie Phillips, DP Plus
Publication design by Wolfgang Bylsma

CONTENTS

For Danny, who keeps my nightmares at bay.

PROLOGUE

The man in the white coat dusted his gloved hands together as if brushing away a fly, letting out a sigh just loud enough to let his colleague know how he felt.

'It's the third time in six months. People are going to start noticing, no matter what steps we take to cover up. If there are endless "equipment malfunctions", then sooner rather than later someone is going to be out here poking around, trying to discern the cause of the malfunction, and they're going to find out.'

His colleague placed a hand on his shoulder. It was not intended to comfort him so much as it was intended to remind him that, if anything happened, they were in the same boat and would sink together. 'Don't let it raise your stress levels,' she said. 'That's not in your job description.'

He laughed in surprise.

'Everything will be all right. I have the PR department working on it already.'

'You don't mean you have so little faith in me that you couldn't wait until she was dead before you acted?'

'No. We merely need to be prepared for every contingency, every situation that may arise. There is nobody better placed to react swiftly than we.' She squeezed his shoulder and then moved away, stripping off her gloves and flicking them expertly into the disposal unit by the door, which immediately roared into action, chewing the latex into nothingness. 'Besides, there is a convenient difference with this one,' she added, as her eyes went to the screen to the left of the door.

'Oh?'

'The family is dead. Killed in a car accident. PR informs me that they were on their way here. The accident has not yet been noted. It will be simple to turn it into a car accident on their way *home* from collecting their beloved daughter.'

The man in the white coat looked down at the pale form lying on the stainless steel table. Eyes closed as if asleep, she appeared untouched. 'Was there a fire?' he asked softly.

'If you like.'

The man in the white coat selected a scalpel from the tray of instruments beside the table. 'I'll hurry.'

'Take your time,' his colleague said, eyes fixed on the lines of text scrolling on the screen, updating the situation. 'We're sending someone straight there to conceal the evidence of the incident until you're ready to make your contribution.'

'I like it when you give me good news,' said the man in the white coat, using the scalpel to remove the dead girl's nightgown with minimal fuss.

'I'm going to go on down to Six and see—' Her words were cut off by the sound of a scream coming from the speaker mounted over the screen. The view abruptly changed from the lines of scrolling text to an image of a white room. A young man was standing in its centre, screaming for no immediately apparent reason.

Get them off me! Get them off!

'His stats are *soaring*,' said the woman.

'Not another one so soon.'

The screaming spiralled up, peaked, and then cut off. The young man in the picture collapsed, sobbing, to the floor. Seconds later a nurse entered the room. He raised his head, managing a watery smile as she spoke soothingly.

'I think I'm getting better at coping,' he told the nurse, his voice tinny through the speaker.

The man in the white coat looked at his colleague. 'Perhaps you'd better go down there after all. He's a healthy specimen. He's bound to be ready for the next stage.'

They both smiled.

CHAPTER ONE

'Erica, can you turn that down, *please*?'

Erica Sayle looked up from the computer monitor. Missy stood in the doorway, one hand on the frame as if for balance. 'Huh? Oh, sorry, possum, I didn't realise it was so loud.' She lowered the volume. 'Better?'

'Yeah. I could hear it from my room.'

'How's the studying going?'

'If I ever see another maths practice exam I'm going to set it on fire.'

'I know what you mean, jellybean. Those things are hell in the form of paper and ink. Did you sleep okay last night?'

'Sort of. I only woke up three times. But ...' Missy hesitated. 'The nightlight was flickering.'

'Oh, possum, it's probably just the globe. Do you want me to change it for you?'

'I can change my own globe. I did it yesterday morning, because it blew during the night. It's not the globe.'

Erica paused the DVD and swivelled around on her chair to face her sister. 'You don't think something's doing it on purpose, do you?' Missy shrugged. 'If it's not the globe, then maybe the wiring's going. Get Dad to look at it.'

'Okay. I mean, I know that it's not really something there—' Missy's thoughts failed her and she flapped one hand helplessly. 'That's just stupid. But sometimes it doesn't seem stupid.'

'Go study, possum. Big week coming up.' Erica watched her sister go back down the hallway to her own room. Missy seemed so fragile sometimes, as if she would snap in half if anyone touched her. The skin under her eyes was frequently touched with dusky purple from lack of sleep; it made her face look even paler, hollowed, as if the skull underneath had surfaced. Her white-blonde hair fell fine and wispy around her face. Ghost hair.

Stop it!

Erica unpaused the DVD. She really had turned it up too loudly. Even if Missy weren't so constantly jumpy, the shrieks and howls from the movie would be distracting. Erica sometimes forgot how hard high school could be; it was long behind her now. And besides, Missy had that other thing to worry about on top of exams. The most Erica had had to worry about in the last week, other than her sister, was whether or not the photocopier was out of toner.

Great. Now she felt guilty for not having *enough* problems.

She watched the rest of the movie, tipped back in her chair so far that she nearly overbalanced it. She could occasionally hear the lawnmower going outside as her father neatened up the back yard, and if he was out there then her mother was probably out there too, weeding or trimming or doing some sort of spring cleanup, ensuring that the dead dry plants were well away from the house before bushfire season started. It was a nice day, though she'd closed the blinds partway to cut the sun-glare on her monitor. Maybe they'd fit in a swim later on if the evening stayed warm, and if the pool lights were working.

Missy woke her up at three the next morning, screaming. Erica stumbled down the hallway and into Missy's room, snapping the overhead light on. Missy was curled into a ball against the head of the bed, staring at nothing, hitching in a breath for another scream. The nightlight had burnt out again. Erica sat down on the edge of the bed and put her arms around her sister, holding her close. Missy's hair still smelled like chlorine. It was the one note that convinced Erica that she was actually awake.

'What if I put the hall light on?' she suggested. 'That should be almost as light as your nightlight, then, and you'll be able to see.'

'You hate having that light on.'

'I can put the door snake down and the light won't come in. It's okay.'

'Is everything all right?' Their father stood just outside the doorway, hesitant.

'It will be,' Erica said. 'I mean, this time next week, exams will be over. I know they gave *me* nightmares.' She felt rather than heard Missy giggling. It was good to know that she could still laugh even after freaking out like that.

'As long as you're sure ...'

'I'm going to put the hall light on. Dad and I are going back to sleep and I suggest you do the same,' Erica said firmly. 'I've got to get up soon.' She kissed the top of Missy's head and stood up. 'We all do.'

Four hours later, Monday morning didn't seem any less surreal. She was getting used to sleepwalking through the first hour or so, and she spent most of that on the bus into work anyway. Missy's first exam wasn't until the afternoon, so at least *she* got to sleep in. The one thing that Erica could clearly remember about high school and most of university was that all of *her* exams had been morning ones.

Doubtless she'd been meant to be learning something from all of her years of schooling beyond the concept of morning exams sucking gnarled hairy monkey balls, but it had all gone right out of her head.

Erica got off the bus and bought a newspaper on her way to work from the bus stop, tucking it into her bag as she crossed the road. She went into work, twitching at her shirt collar and smoothing the train-seat-rumples out of her skirt as she walked through the automatic doors. One of the program directors was looking for a PA, and if she was lucky, the interview would be today. If she was unlucky, then she'd spend another six weeks loading printer paper and answering the phone before something else came up. Not that she minded doing office work. She was putting most of her money into a savings account anyway. She'd worry about getting a classier job when she could afford to move to a suburb where there *were* classier jobs. Although PA to a radio station program director sounded all right, the fact that it was a country radio station that had reception in only a small area made it less impressive. Still, she was lucky enough to have parents who didn't mind her staying at home until she had the money to go where she wanted to go, and there was usually enough left out of her pay each fortnight to buy a new DVD or book.

She'd bought a lot of DVDs and books in her time, as a matter of fact. The walls of her bedroom were lined with shelves piled high with Stephen King novels, Dean Koontz novels, the entire Fear Street series (from her younger years), and dozens of horror DVDs. Erica was a horror fanatic, and Missy was her exact opposite. Erica had never been able to plough through *The Lord of the Rings* even once, making it as far as the Council of Elrond before slamming the book shut in disgust, but Missy reread it once a year, always in winter, curled up on the floor near the central heating duct in her room with a doona and pillows making a nest. Erica's winter reread was *The Stand,* because it added to the atmosphere during flu season. And she always looked forward to October, when the horror movies hit the cinemas for Halloween, whereas

Missy liked nothing better than to dress up for the *Harry Potter* movie opening nights.

Erica dropped her bag behind the reception desk and spread out her newspaper, then went back into the tearoom to get a cup of tea. She had an hour before the front door would open, and it wasn't as if they got many visitors, but there might be phone messages to note down off the answering machine.

Brad from the morning team was in the tearoom, shoving coins into the vending machine as fast as he could as an ad for a car dealership played over the speakers that were everywhere in the building. He gave her a quick wave and smile as he scooped up his bag of cheese and onion chips and hurried back to the studio. For a small radio station, everyone got a lot of bustling around done. Except Erica. She sometimes wondered why they bothered having a receptionist.

Tea made, Erica sat down at her desk, started the computer, and checked the machine for messages. One message, but the caller said nothing—it sounded like they'd been standing in a high wind, and maybe they hadn't heard the beep or something. Erica deleted it.

That was about the most exciting thing that happened all day. She didn't get her interview, which meant that she was going to have to keep dressing up until she did. She wrote job ads in her head:

Wanted: Someone who will sit behind a desk all day, answer the phone twice, and otherwise be bored out of their skull. Must be willing to clean the coffee machine, including the skanky milk hoses, and consequently smell like off milk for the rest of the day because the soap dispensers in the toilets didn't get refilled again. Must also like photocopier toner, especially having it all over their hands. Willingness to smile and nod when the program directors stop by your desk to talk about 'nash' and 'reeg' ratings because they're oh-so-hip optional. Salary package: might not be big bucks, but you get Internet access and it almost never gets checked because everyone else in the office is computer illiterate due to being older than God.

Maybe she could just talk Missy into doing her job over summer and worry about replacing her when the next school year rolled around. Except Missy already had her own job; she was a counter girl at the local chicken shop. Damn. She'd have to leave it up to the company to replace her. If she ever got promoted, that was. If she ever got out from behind this desk.

Erica had been working reception for almost a year, since she had finished her degree and immediately started job hunting and gotten lucky because the previous receptionist had quit in a fit of boredom. She was beginning to understand just how unsatisfying getting paid to sit around all day doing nothing actually was. The bright side was that, since she spent all day at work online, it freed up time at home to watch DVDs and read books. Not to mention that there was a certain degree of satisfaction in job-hunting from a work computer.

Five o'clock rolled around just as Erica was contemplating how damned shallow she could be at times. She shut the computer down, turned the answering machine on, and stuffed the newspaper back into her bag; the usual sequence of mundane events got her home, where Missy was telling their parents excitedly about how well her English exam had gone and the whole house smelled of roasting chicken.

She sat by Missy's bed that night and talked to her about the exam and about Saturday. Missy, in her own quiet way, was getting quite hyped up about the appointment. The Centralia Fear Clinic was relatively new—six months or so—and they had waited until they had heard favourable reviews of the work done there before making Missy's preliminary assessment appointment.

Doctor Chapman, the woman who had taken Missy's details, had seemed very optimistic about Missy's potential for treatment.

'Fear of the dark is more common than most people realise,' she had explained, sitting behind her wide wooden desk and smiling across it at the family. 'It's even got multiple names, although the one we generally use here is *nyctophobia*, because it so frequently goes hand in hand with a fear of the night.'

She went on to say that she understood that Missy wasn't really afraid of the dark so much as she was afraid of what might be *in* the dark. She said nothing about it being silly for a seventeen-year-old to be afraid of the dark, as one of the other therapists Missy had seen implied. In fact, flipping through the pamphlet provided by the clinic, Erica had seen that quite a lot of the patients who had written anonymous recommendations were even older than Missy, and some of them had phobias that she'd never even imagined. Rats and spiders and snakes were a given, but puppets? Telephones? *Frogs*?

Yes, Missy was hyped; thrilled at the idea of being able to find some sort of cure, at the thought of being able to sleep through the night without waking the whole household by screaming her head off in terror at some imagined-real threat.

'Possum, you're not going to get to sleep *tonight* if you don't calm down,' Erica said.

'I will. Really. I wore my brain all out studying for English, but it was worth it.'

'Good. Goodnight.' Erica went to her own room, wondering what time she'd be woken this night.

To her surprise, Missy didn't bring the house down that night. Or the next, or the next. It seemed as if the hope of a cure so close had taken the edge off her nightmares. She breezed through her exams one by one, until at last it was Friday night and she pushed her chair back from the table after dinner and blithely announced, 'I'm going to a post-exams party.'

'Where?' their mother asked.

'Aaron's place. He's invited everyone over.'

'Aaron as in Aaron Noonan or as in Aaron Robertson?' Erica asked.

'Noonan.'

'I can drive her over and hang out with Toby for a while and bring her home if you want,' Erica offered to her parents, who were looking dubious.

'Really? That would be so cool!' Missy said. 'I didn't really want to ask, I was going to get the bus over, but that would be cool.'

'Oh, all right,' their mother said. 'Just be home by midnight—we have to be at the clinic tomorrow, don't forget.'

'Mum, the appointment's at *four*,' Missy said.

'Midnight,' Mrs. Sayle repeated.

'*Fine!*'

Erica cleared the table while Missy bounded upstairs to get ready to go out. She was showing more exuberance than she had in weeks, probably due to the end of exams; she had months to go before she had to start her final year of school.

It was only a short drive to the Noonans' house, but on foot it would be a long way on dark streets. In the car there was music, and the lights from the dashboard, and company. As they passed looming trees and dark driveway entrances gaping between them like toothless mouths with long dirt tongues, Erica could almost see why Missy got so afraid.

Not to mention that the bus stopped at the end of the Noonans' driveway, which was convenient. But then it would be a five-minute walk up said driveway, which was not at all well lit, with branches that waved in the wind, reaching out and scraping along the side of the car when Erica drifted too far to one side. All in all, she was glad that at least it wasn't a Halloween party. Missy didn't do too well with those.

Erica parked the car to one side of the wide gravelled turnaround so she and Missy could walk to the front door together. Inside, Missy vanished into the gaggle of kids crowding the living room, while Erica headed straight upstairs to Toby's room.

He was sitting by the window, staring into the night, a notepad resting forgotten on his knees.

'Hey,' Erica said.

'Hey.' He turned to face her. 'Tonight would be a great night for a bonfire.'

'Isn't it a total fire ban?'

'Not yet. I'm sure my brother will get it organised before long.' Toby put the notepad on his desk and tucked his knees closer to his chest, making space for Erica on the window seat. She sat without having to be asked.

'How's the writing?' Erica asked.

'Slow, but I don't mind. Deadline's next Friday. I've got forever.'

'You've got a *week*,' Erica corrected.

'It's not as if I can't whip something up at the last minute if need be.'

Erica rolled her eyes. 'I haven't forgotten that you're the local boy wonder reporter.'

'Did you read the article I did about the housing zoning plan down near—'

'Yeah, it's not good for any residents who aren't ducks, I got it. *I was looking for real estate for us.*'

'The big city,' Toby said dreamily.

'Bigger and better job opportunities.'

'No greenery, though.'

'And people assuming we're a couple. Let's table this discussion for another three months.'

'We can't wait much longer; I think Mum wants me out of home before I turn eighty.'

They sat in companionable silence, looking out of the window at the party-goers as they swarmed out of the house and into the backyard, building a stack of wood that would throw an endless flame into the sky if it were lit carefully. Erica could see Missy directing the stacking of the wood, forming it into a chimney that would funnel the flame upwards until it collapsed in upon itself.

'She didn't learn that from Guides,' Toby commented.

'No. She learned how to make neat campfires for cooking over from Guides. She learned how to make big bonfires from *you*.'

'I am a man of many talents.' Toby winked. 'What time's the appointment tomorrow?'

'Four. Although looking at the way she's doing now, it's hard to believe that there's anything wrong. She's just so confident.'

'She's staying within reach of the veranda lights, though,' Toby pointed out. 'She's not going into the shadows for wood.'

The flame roared up through the piled branches; Erica could faintly hear the kids cheering. Someone ran into the house and re-emerged with a bag of marshmallows.

'Apparently they have a really high success rate.' Erica twisted a strand of her hair around her fingers. 'I'd settle for knowing that she'll be able to sleep through the night, every night.'

'There are people who don't sleep through the night every night who don't have crippling phobias.'

'Toby ...'

'I know, I know. I'm glad that there's someone who can help Missy. I just wish that someone could help Mum. She always looks so exhausted, and she's defending some scumbag at the moment and she's sure he's guilty, but she has to act like he's not. It sucks.'

Erica reached out and patted his hand. 'I can always ask when we go up there tomorrow if they know anyone who deals with insomnia. We thought there was nothing left that could help Missy, and then this turned up.'

'Good. Yeah. Thanks.' Toby rubbed breath-fog off the window. 'I think we should go down there.'

'Oh, I think they're pretty responsible. Don't you?'

'Yeah, of course. But I could really go a marshmallow or two right about now.' Toby got to his feet and held out a hand to Erica, who took it and got up. 'Come on, or all the pink ones will be gone.'

Chapter Two

The car crunched on the gravel driveway in front of the single-storey white building, pulling into one of the parking spaces near the sign with the red arrow pointing to RECEPTION. Their parents got out first, walking straight to the front entrance of the clinic. Missy hesitated, one hand on the doorhandle, the other drumming against her denim-clad knee.

'Come on, possum,' Erica said. 'Glory awaits.'

Missy gave her a wavering smile and opened the car door. Her confidence of the previous night had burnt out like the bonfire; she walked to the clinic's entrance with her head down. Erica slid out of the car, slammed her door (it sometimes didn't shut properly), and followed.

The first part of the clinic was familiar from their last visit. The front door opened onto a long hallway with doors at regular intervals, but immediately to the left was the waiting area, with soft cream leather couches that had to cost a fortune just to keep clean, and the long polished wooden reception desk. The walls were the exact same shade of cream as the couches. Erica imagined that every colour, every piece of furniture in the place, had been especially selected as the most soothing option, to calm its fearful clients.

Even Cynthia, the receptionist, was soothing. Comfortably round in face and body, she had brown hair and eyes that sparkled when she smiled her warm, inviting smile. Erica smiled back. So did Missy. So did their parents.

'Melissa Sayle. Welcome back. Are you ready for your first treatment?'

Missy nodded.

'Do you want to make a cup of tea or coffee before you go through?' Cynthia looked at all four of them, including them all in the query. Erica nodded this time, and Cynthia smiled again. 'The tea things are just over there.' She waved one hand to the table set up with its gently steaming urn, neat white bowls of teabags and coffee and Milo and sugar with silver spoons poking out of them, and tiny fridge humming away as it kept three kinds of milk cool. 'I'll let Doctor Chapman know that you're here, but I believe she's already got your room prepared.'

Erica made tea for everyone—sweet and milky for herself, black for her mother and father, white but sugarless for Missy, who didn't like to entirely drown the taste of the tea out with other flavours. Missy sat with her suitcase beside her and sipped slowly. Erica drank her first cup of tea so fast that she had to make another one, or be the only one sitting there with an empty cup when the doctor arrived.

It wasn't long before Doctor Chapman came striding into the reception area from somewhere down the long hallway, smiling, arm already extended to shake hands all around.

'Welcome, welcome,' she said. 'Melissa, your room is ready and waiting for you. There are a few forms to fill out and a couple more preliminary tests to go through, but we've just about settled on what your initial treatment level will be.' Missy started to rise to her feet; Doctor Chapman pushed her back down with a light touch on one shoulder. 'No, no, finish your drink first, there's no rush.' She moved to the urn and made herself a coffee.

Missy finished her drink, watching Erica over the rim of the cup. She was clearly trying hard not to appear nervous, but Erica had grown up with her, known her all her life, and knew the little signs that gave Missy's moods away.

'We've roughed out a program of treatment, if you want to see it,' Doctor Chapman said. 'But it's basically what we told you initially—beginning with a low level of exposure and analysing Melissa's responses, and building it all up from there. We'll do a lot of work to find out why exactly Melissa is having the reactions that she does, and then we can treat the cause— whether it's a subconscious connection or something else, we *will* find out, and we *will* fix it.' She gave their parents a professional smile. Erica caught Missy's eye, rolled hers: adult speak in action, talking over their heads as if they weren't there.

'Well,' Mr. Sayle said, 'it all sounds very reasonable.' He rose to his feet. 'We should let you get on with it.'

'No rush,' Doctor Chapman repeated.

'I'm ready,' Missy said.

'Thank you, Mr. and Mrs. Sayle,' Doctor Chapman said.

'Richard and Diana, please.'

Doctor Chapman nodded, apparently filing their names away for future use in some corner of her mind, but didn't offer her own first name.

'Don't forget, you're more than welcome to visit between ten and two each day, but as we continue treatments during the day for some patients as well as at night, depending on the nature of their phobia, we do ask that you not come outside of those hours without an appointment. But of course there's always the phone, and you can reach us any time if there's a personal emergency at home.' She looked at Missy. 'Ready to go?'

Missy made the rounds, hugging each of them goodbye. She came to Erica last and held onto her for a long moment.

'You'll be fine, possum,' Erica said softly.

'I know.' Missy's grip tightened briefly, and then she let go, stepped back, and picked up her suitcase. 'It's only a week.'

Still, when Erica glanced back as she and her parents were leaving the building, Missy seemed very small as she went along the long hallway with Doctor Chapman, her shoulders hunched, her head lowered, the straps of her bag twisted around her hand as if she were clinging onto her only connection to the outside world, afraid that it would disappear and she wouldn't be able to get back to reality.

You're being ridiculous. You can't tell all of that from here.

Still, Erica resolved to visit as often as she could. It was only a half hour drive from home, she had her own car, and work got so slow at times that they probably wouldn't even notice if she wasn't there. And as Doctor Chapman had said, there was always the phone. Not that Missy would have one in her own room, because that would probably be disruptive to the treatment, but she wasn't lying immobile in a regular hospital; she could get up and walk to the reception desk if she wanted to. That was the thing to remember. Everything was nice and normal and in a few hours her sister would begin her first treatment and then everything would be fine for her.

Oh balls!

Wherever this negative voice was coming from, Erica wanted it to shut the hell up.

She called Toby when she got home and he came over immediately, sprawling comfortably on the banana lounge next to hers out by the pool. The hot weather was really starting to gear up, but Erica would forever be grateful that her parents had been able to afford to make the pool heatable, especially for those times when the weather changed suddenly in the middle of a swim and the rain blew in from nowhere.

'So what's the place like?'

'They painted it cream. I guess if they went with stark white it'd be too hospital-ly. I would have picked nicer couches if I were their interior designer.'

'How about Missy's room?'

'We didn't get to see that. They like their clients to be able to settle themselves in first before they allow the families in.'

'Huh.' Toby considered the situation for a minute, and then added, 'Weird.'

'Yeah, I know.'

'So when are you going to go visit her?'

'Maybe tomorrow. I don't know how I'm going to manage during the week. I've got work every day, but I could pull a sickie on Wednesday or something so at least she doesn't go all week alone.'

'Just don't say that in front of your parents,' Toby said. 'They'll rat you out.'

'They wouldn't. Not if I'm doing it for Missy.'

'I got another full chapter done last night—this morning, I mean—after you guys went home. I think the marshmallows helped. Sugar is good writing fuel.'

'Toby, you're meant to be working on that article about the swimming pool getting closed down, not writing your book.'

'Inspiration doesn't strike every day, my dear,' Toby said loftily. 'You should try writing when you're at work, instead of spending all day on Facebook.'

'And neglect my movie trivia team? Never.'

'Because it's okay to neglect our Scrabble game?'

'Okay, you know what?' Erica got up and ducked inside for a moment, pulling her ancient Scrabble set off the games shelf beside the TV. 'We can play Scrabble right here and now if it will make you feel better.'

Toby gestured at the pool, the water still and clear and blue in the late afternoon sunlight. 'You don't want to swim?'

'Not yet.' Erica set the board up and drew her tiles. 'We can swim anytime. This is clearly more important to you.'

'You know I'm just going to kick your arse.'

'Yes. Yes, you are. Because you're a journalist and a writer and I'm just a receptionist who spends all day reading webcomics.' Erica laid out her tiles, spelling QUALITY. 'I don't know any big words that are worth loads of points at all.'

Toby stared at the board. 'Huh. How about that.'

Erica smirked and handed him the bag of tiles. 'Beat that, wordsmith.'

Toby shook the bag and arranged seven tiles on the rack in front of him, leaning forward to study them closely. 'Prepare to be beaten, oh dark lady of infinite horrors.'

'That would explain why I don't have a boyfriend,' Erica said dryly.

Toby put down LAMA under Erica's L. 'Don't say that.'

'You know I don't mean it like that.'

'*I* never complain about not having a boyfriend,' Toby said smugly.

'That's just a tiny bit different, wouldn't you say?' Erica drew another set of tiles and groaned when she saw how many consonants she had pulled. 'Crap.'

Toby recognised her tone of voice. 'Rhythm. Tryst. Syzygy.'

'I haven't got any ... oh, wait.' She put down an L, N, and X, to spell LYNX with the Y from QUALITY. 'There.'

They played the game through; in the end, Toby won, but only by fifteen points.

'I'm getting better at this,' Erica said with satisfaction.

'You are.' Toby got up. 'Let's swim.'

'Hang on; I've got to pack this up first.'

Toby picked the board up, tiles and all, and carried it inside, dumping it on the coffee table. 'Happy?'

Erica pulled her shirt and shorts off, revealing her hibiscus-patterned bathers. 'Eminently. Thank you.' She padded barefoot around the pool to the deep end and stepped up onto the low board her Dad had had put in so Missy could practice diving when she was in year nine and the swimming carnival was the highlight of the school summer calendar. The blue ribbon she'd won was still hanging up in the pool room. Erica herself was never going to win any awards for diving or swimming, but when she was twelve she'd won an icypole for splashiest dive-bomb at their local pool. She leapt off the low board, tucking her knees up to her chest, and hit the water with maximum impact, sending water flying everywhere and a medium-sized wave rolling up to where Toby was edging his way gingerly into the water at the shallow end.

'I keep telling you, it's not cold,' Erica said when she surfaced. 'I can turn the heat up for you if you want.'

'Old habits die hard.'

Erica duck-dived back under and swam for his legs; Toby, seeing her coming, splashed hastily back up the steps. 'Maybe I should sit in the spa for a few minutes and get used to it,' he suggested.

'There's nothing to get used to! The water's twenty-five degrees!'

'Oh, well, then,' said Toby, and he threw himself into the water, spraying water into Erica's face and almost catching her legs before she twisted away. She went back under the water, hugging the wall and staying close to the bottom, trying to sneak up on him—wherever he'd gone.

A hand closed around her left ankle and tugged. A fingertip began tickling the sole of her right foot. Erica lost her breath in a mass of bubbles and surfaced, spluttering—Toby had let go as soon as he saw that she was trying to go up. The one thing that they were always careful not to do was genuinely endanger each other. It seemed obvious enough, but to them was even more important since they had both nearly drowned, aged ten, when a riptide caught them trying to swim to the pier and back on a beach trip.

Half an hour of roughhousing was all that both of them could manage; after that, Erica sprawled on her stomach on the dive platform and tossed weighted, coloured plastic rings into the water for Toby to retrieve. Now he didn't want to come out, because the sunlight was fading and the water was warmer than the air.

Erica's father came out of the house. 'Toby, are you staying for dinner?' he asked.

'Only if you're having something nice,' Toby said.

Erica pushed his head under the water with her foot. 'He'll stay,' she said. 'Do you want a hand with anything?'

'No, your mother's got the salad under control, and I checked that the barbecue was cleaned out last weekend. I just wanted to know how many sausages to do.' The barbecue was an imposing brick fireplace that Toby called 'the incinerator', and that wasn't an unfair description, given that Erica's father often used it to burn off any dead branches that he cleared out of the garden.

'Did you get garlic ones again?'

'And those little ones with the cheese and tomato.'

'You're staying,' Erica informed Toby, who had surfaced, spluttering. 'There're chipolatas.'

'Yum. We'll need another swim after dinner to work it all off again.'

Erica slipped off the diving platform into the water. 'We could pre-emptively exercise,' she said.

Toby was already kicking off the wall, and she had to stretch to catch up, but she still touched the other end before he did. He was the brain; she was the brawn; they would have made a great couple if only they hadn't been so perfectly well matched. Matches like that simply did not exist outside of fiction.

Besides, he was *Toby*.

They did laps for another five minutes but lost interest as the smell of barbecuing sausages and burgers rose on the air. Before much longer both of them were out of the pool, wrapping thick towels around themselves, and making a move for the picnic table.

'You could always help by setting that, you know,' Erica's mother said, bringing out the salad bowl.

Erica jumped back up and went inside for a handful of cutlery. Toby followed her and brought out a stack of plates without Erica asking.

Missy and Aaron were once as close, but as Missy's phobia had grown worse she had stopped going out at night. Now that Erica came to think of it, she didn't think Missy had ever been as close to anyone as she was to Toby. It wasn't fair. Erica had lived long enough to know that friends often came and went, but surely everyone needed at least one really good, close friend? Maybe *she* was Missy's best friend; she certainly tried to be as much of a friend as she could, rather than just being her big sister.

Erica decided that she was going to see Missy the next day, even though visiting on the second day of

Missy's treatment seemed very early. Still, she'd get to see the room where Missy was staying and maybe she'd get a better idea of exactly what Missy's treatment entailed. There had been buzzwords bandied about, such as 'cognitive-behavioural therapy' and 'high-intensity, tightly focussed phobia treatments based upon increasing exposure to stimuli', but whether that meant that Missy went into the room and they turned the lights off and then waited for her to start screaming and wrote it all down, or whether there was something more active involved, Erica wasn't quite certain. Doctor Chapman had said that there were a number of different treatment pathways.

'Earth to Erica ... Earth to Erica ... come in, Erica ...' Toby was waving a tomato and cheese chipolata under her nose. She snapped at it; Toby withdrew it and stuffed it whole into his own mouth. 'What were you thinking about?'

'Just Missy,' Erica said. 'I might go and visit her tomorrow.'

'Are you sure it's a good idea to go in so soon?' her mother asked. 'I know they don't mind visitors sometimes, but she's only just gone in.'

'I won't be able to visit her during the week unless I get time off work,' Erica pointed out. 'You guys have more flexibility than I do.'

Since her father was a lawyer who had been known to work twenty-hour days, and her mother was a freelance accountant who ran her own business out of her study, it was only half true, but her mother nodded anyway. 'Fair enough. Just stick to their visiting hours.'

'Ten 'til two, I know. I wasn't planning on spending all day there.' Erica speared a sausage with her fork and plopped it onto a piece of bread, drizzling it with tomato sauce. 'I just want to see how Missy's doing, that's all.'

Toby left at about ten o'clock and Erica wandered up to her bedroom, booting the computer up and scanning her DVD shelves to try and pick something to watch before bed. Eventually she settled on *IT*, set the movie running, and curled up in her computer chair. The computer, tricked out with a huge monitor and about a million gigabytes of hard drive space, had been her birthday present for her twenty-first; she mostly used it as a substitute television because nobody else in the house appreciated her taste in movies.

The swimming had worn her out, and her head sagged slowly down onto her shoulder, her eyes drooping closed.

She was walking down a long corridor, following someone wearing a white lab coat. They turned in at a door marked simply with a gold numeral: 8. The door was painted cream. The room was painted cream, and the bed in the middle of the room had pale blue sheets.

Two doors opened off the room; she caught a glimpse of a shower stall and toilet through one. The other door was closed. The words TREATMENT ROOM were written on a small plaque on the closed door. The words made her nervous.

'We can begin as soon as you're settled in,' said the person in the white lab coat.

'I need to go to the—the—' She inclined her head towards the bathroom door; it was the sound of her voice, which was not her usual voice, that made Erica realise that she was someone else. It was a small voice, as if its owner were afraid to speak up.

She went into the bathroom, used the toilet, and went to wash her hands at the basin. There was a small mirror mounted over the basin, and she saw a timid face, framed with lank brown hair. A nondescript face. A face she probably wouldn't recognise if she saw it again.

The door to the treatment room was open when she returned to the main room, and the person in the white lab coat was in there, waiting.

'We'll begin the procedure now, shall we?'

She went into the room and stood next to the person in the white lab coat, who held out a soft calico bag to her.

'This isn't part of the treatment,' she said, her voice shaky.

'It will help you isolate the source of the fear,' the person told her gently, 'if you cut off all external stimuli.' The person reached out and placed the bag over her head. The bag stuck to her face as she inhaled. The bag was only the size of her head to begin with, but as it was pulled down over her, it grew. It went over her head, her shoulders, down to her waist, down to her feet, and suddenly it wasn't calico but rough black plastic, and she heard the sound of a zipper closing.

'Extraction successful,' said a computerised voice from nowhere. 'Treatment complete. Subject deceased.'

'That's two,' said a female voice. 'We can't afford any more mistakes.'

Erica's hands went to her face as she woke up, but there was nothing there except one of those weird indented patterns from sleeping on clothing. The scariest thing in the room was Tim Curry capering across the screen as Pennywise, and since Erica personally thought he was scarier in drag as Frank-N-Furter, she suddenly felt very embarrassed. Was that how Missy felt when she woke up scared? Upset that she'd been scared by a dream, or too busy being terrified to worry about how she appeared to others?

She stopped the DVD and shut the computer down. If she were so tired that she fell asleep sitting up, then it was time to shower the chlorine out of her hair and go to bed. She went into the bathroom that she and Missy shared and looked in the mirror. Whoever the girl in the mirror had been in the dream, it wasn't her. Erica's hair was blonde, like Missy's only yellower, and the only reason that it hung limply around her face was that she hadn't dried it after swimming. Moreover, she didn't look pale and afraid in the least. In fact, her cheeks had burned a bit during the day because she'd forgotten to put sunscreen on.

'You're not afraid of anything,' she reminded her reflection. 'Missy's afraid of everything for you.' She turned away from the mirror and got the shower running, shedding her shirt, shorts, and mostly-dry bathers once the water had heated up. She glanced back at the mirror once before getting into the shower, but it was still her.

As she shampooed her hair, Erica's mind returned to her earlier thought: was this how Missy felt all the time? Jumping at shadows and sudden out of place movements, always wondering whether there was something or someone under the bed or in the wardrobe, listening for every odd sound in the middle of the night until at last she fell into an uneasy sleep, only to wake up screaming from yet another nightmare? Missy's phobia was a perfect example of an irrational fear, because nothing bad had ever happened to her.

Erica was the one who had nearly drowned when she was a child; Erica was the one who read books and watched movies about all the bad things that can happen when mundane life turns to something horrifyingly warped; Erica was the one who had given in and learned to drive so that she could get to Toby's because it was safer than being followed home from the bus stop at the end of their street by a stranger in an unmarked white van.

Missy didn't have any reason to be afraid of the dark, or of anything that might or might not be lurking in it. Erica tried hard not to get irritated about it, and managed quite well most of the time. It was just that being woken up at three in the morning several nights running got wearisome, and her parents' bedroom was further down the hall towards the stairs, so she was the one who heard Missy first every single time.

She'd mused about the exact same thing every so often for the past three years. Missy had started out by coming down to the breakfast table looking a little peaky every other morning. Then she'd started sleeping with the bathroom light on and the door open, until that wasn't enough and she had to have the nightlight right by her bed, because the light from the bathroom didn't quite reach the furthest corners of her room. The nightlight was small, but with a hundred-watt globe in it, it was enough to keep the darkness at bay. To Erica's surprise the light Missy had chosen was a clown; she found it soothing, but it just reminded Erica of Pennywise.

But finally the monsters had broken through from the darkness of night into the darkness behind Missy's eyelids, and the flood of nightmares had begun, and nothing worked—not valerian, not sleeping pills, not warm milk before bed, nothing.

They had seen various specialists, of course. A psychologist who tried to establish, quite unfairly, which of their parents was being abusive. Another psychologist who, though she identified and found ways to alleviate Missy's school-related stress, didn't stop the nightmares. A dream interpreter. A sleep specialist, who checked for sleep apnoea and other physical problems and didn't understand that, unless there really *was* someone hanging off Missy's windowsill every night and tapping on the glass with their fingernails, there wasn't actually anything physical to cure. An aromatherapist—Missy's room, and consequently most of the hallway, smelled like lavender for weeks.

But none of it worked.

Then the Centralia Fear Clinic had opened up in the next town over, and they heard favourable things about its success rate, and though it was a facility with very few beds—'we like to make sure our patient to staff ratio remains one to at least one,' Doctor Morley had said—they had found a place for Missy. Immediately, in fact.

Either it was the fact that the clinic was still relatively unheard of and they were out in the sticks and so the staff hadn't filled all the beds yet, or it was something to do with Richard Sayle's wallet. Erica favoured the former explanation, although she knew it would only be a matter of time before every second person who had even the mildest fear of, say, flying would be fighting for a place.

The reported success rate had been *extremely* high, and results like that were worth travelling out of the city for an hour and a half or whatever it was. Erica figured there were probably enough therapists and psychologists and that sort of thing to cover most of the people who lived in the city and had problems, which had to be nearly all of them, considering they were living in the city—she couldn't imagine living in a tiny apartment with the nearest thing to a garden being a little potted fern out on the foot-wide balcony. She couldn't imagine living anywhere but Lilywood, even if it was a stupid name for a town (she secretly hoped that one day the town boundaries would change and then she'd be living in Centralia, because although Centralia was a pretty stupid name too, it had connotations that she, as a horror fan, couldn't possibly dislike).

Erica realised that her fingers and toes were going pruny and turned the shower off. She got out and dried herself and wiped the steam off the mirror, mildly disappointed when the face in the mirror was hers and not that of some leering monster or the strange girl from her dream, and pulled her nightie on over her head after towelling her hair dry.

Nothing horrible happened to her even after calling goodnight to her parents and settling into bed with Christopher Pike's *Witch*. It was almost a shame. Erica had often felt that she might get even more out of her horror stories if she were actually frightened by them. It was a fairly uncharitable thought considering

Missy's condition, but she couldn't help thinking it anyway.

She finished reading the book and turned the light off.

Nothing went bump in the night.

CHAPTER THREE

Erica got to the clinic at half past eleven the next morning and noted quite a few cars already parked outside. As she went in, a group of three people passed her on their way to their car—a guy, maybe a year older than Missy, who was pale but smiling, and an older couple who were presumably his parents.

'—happy to be able to come home,' she caught the guy saying.

'We're just happy that you won't—' that was the woman, but Erica didn't catch the end of the sentence. Still, it seemed like they were going home as satisfied customers, and that was the main thing.

She went into reception. Cynthia was there again; she looked up and saw Erica and immediately pushed a button on a panel behind the desk.

'Hello?' Missy's voice buzzed through a speaker.

'Hi, Melissa; your sister's here to see you.'

'Cool, thanks, I'll be right out.'

Cynthia smiled at Erica. 'You're a good sister, coming out here on a weekend to visit.'

'Yeah, well, I can't do weekdays without getting someone to cover for me at work. I'm sure you know what that's like.'

'Oh, believe me, I'm always *real* happy when someone comes to replace me.' Cynthia glanced around, lowered her voice, and added, 'It gets kind of boring 'cause we're usually pretty quiet, you know?'

Erica laughed. 'I know *exactly* what you mean.'

Missy came into the waiting area, looking a little nervous but pleased to see her sister. 'Is it okay if I show her my room now?' she asked Cynthia.

'Hi, possum,' Erica said.

'Hi,' Missy said, turning immediately back to Cynthia. 'Is it? Otherwise we can go into the garden or something.'

'Erica might want to see your room *and* the garden,' Cynthia said. 'That's fine.' She handed Erica a VISITOR tag, which Erica pinned to the front of her blue halter top. 'The staff know all our clients by sight, but not everyone knows all of the families. Keep that on and you'll be able to go anywhere that Melissa can go.'

Missy led Erica down the hallway to a room almost all the way down the end. The doors were widely spaced, and each had a number on them in gold, except for the odd room labelled CLEANING SUPPLIES CLOSET or EMERGENCY EXIT–DOOR IS ALARMED. Missy's room was number twelve. She opened the door and went in. Erica followed, and stopped stock-still into the doorway as she saw the cream walls, the pale blue sheets on the bed, and the two other doors leading out of the room.

'I dreamed about this place last night,' she managed to say eventually.

Missy turned, frowning a little. 'What?'

'I had a dream that I was here. Not here this room—it was a different number—but it was the same sort of room with the same layout.'

'Well, you must've seen one of the rooms yesterday or when we came for that first appointment or something,' Missy said, sitting down on the edge of the bed. 'They had a few doors open around the place. I got breakfast in bed today. Maybe if you did that at home I'd get better.' She gave Erica a cheeky smile that Erica hadn't seen for months.

'Smartarse,' Erica said automatically, but her eyes were on the other two doors. One said BATHROOM. The other said TREATMENT ROOM. 'What's in those two rooms?'

Missy gave her an odd look. 'It says right on the doors. Did you forget how to read?'

'No, but what's *in* the treatment room?'

'Just the computer and stuff they use to simulate trigger situations. I'd show you, but they lock it during the day. I think so they can set up the next simulation without being interrupted.'

'What's it like?'

Missy shrugged. 'Okay, I guess. Most of the session was tests to see if anything in particular triggered my fear responses—they put electrodes on me and put a thing on my finger and then I sat at the computer and they showed a bunch of pictures and played sounds and measured stuff like how much I sweated and if my heart rate went up and all that. I feel like a psych experiment, only not as bad as the ones they used to do. That stuff gives me the willies. I should've told them about that—all the morally questionable experiments back in the sixties and seventies, before they invented ethics.'

'I can't believe you're studying psychology,' Erica said without thinking.

Missy shrugged again. 'I think it's good for me to try and confront this stuff. Plus I keep thinking maybe I'll find something that will help.'

'I guess that's true.'

'They ruled out any other phobias from the tests, but I knew that anyway. They show spiders and snakes and the view from an open airplane door and that as well. I think maybe everyone gets this first set of images and sounds and then gradually they customise it. Their DVD library's probably as big as yours. Probably got a bunch of the same stuff in it, too.' Missy smiled. 'I recognised some of the pictures from your movies. That clown puppet thing from that really gory movie, and the mask from *Scream*. I get why people would be scared of those. They're pretty freaky. I'm still not sure about the frog thing though.'

'I doubt anyone here's *really* got a phobia of frogs. I think they made that up,' Erica said. 'I don't think anyone would want to admit to it. I wouldn't, if it were me.'

'Yeah, well, pretty much any phobia looks stupid if you're not the one who has it.'

'So what else did they do?'

'Not much. I had to keep the electrodes on while I slept, and they were measuring my brainwaves and kept waking me up when I went into dreaming sleep to ask if I could remember what I was dreaming about.'

'And could you?'

'Sort of. I had this one dream about being at our house and hearing something weird while I was playing Tetris on the computer and getting freaked out and then realising it was Dad snoring, but that's pretty boring. I think they were expecting, like, dreams about the zombie uprising, or vampires attacking people, or something a bit more dire than *snoring*.'

'Well, maybe you'll have a really horrendous nightmare tonight to make up for it,' Erica suggested.

Missy stuck her tongue out. 'Come on, let's go see the garden. You'll like it. It's a bit of a mess.'

Erica did indeed like the garden. The lawn was neatly trimmed, dotted here and there with tables sprouting large sun-umbrellas, surrounded by folding chairs that looked as rickety as the furniture down at their beach place on the coast (their father kept meaning to buy new chairs, but forgot every year until they were down there, and then decided that they could make do with the existing ones for just one more summer). In contrast to the lawn, though, the flowers were creeping over the edge of the rock borders, threatening to escape and start attacking the patients, a few of whom were sitting at the tables. Some of them were drinking tea, others just staring off at nothing.

'It's lucky nobody's afraid of plants,' Erica whispered. She took another look at the people in the garden. Most of them looked all right, but there were a few who seemed really out of it. 'None of them *are* afraid of plants, right?'

'I don't think so. Not everyone talks about it, though. I know one of the guys is afraid of spiders, and one of the girls is afraid of heights, but I think people are scared to discuss it in case they get made fun of.'

'God, why? You're all here for treatment. You're all afraid of something.'

'Yes, but it's not necessarily something that makes sense. That's why a phobia is an *irrational* fear. It's not like if you were afraid of drowning, because that would make sense, given what happened when you were ten.'

'You remember that?'

'I remember Mum screaming, and Dad dragging you out of the water, and Mr. Noonan froze up so Dad had to go back in after Toby as well.'

'I don't remember all that. I just remember my arms got tired, so I floated.'

'I'm glad you floated,' Missy said, giving her an unexpected hug.

Erica hugged her back. 'You'll float right through this too, don't worry.'

'I think so too. It doesn't seem like that much of a big deal, but apparently it works.' Missy let go. 'Come on, there are some really pretty pansies down the other end of the garden.'

Erica followed her sister past the picnic tables, smiling at the people sitting there. She noticed that two of them were staff members, wearing pale blue polo shirts with the clinic's logo above the left chest pocket. It certainly wasn't the one to one ratio that had been mentioned, but maybe that was just for actual treatment. They were probably only outside in case someone had an unexpected reaction to something in the garden. Pansies could be pretty terrifying, after all.

Up close, the garden beds were in pretty poor shape. The flowers were blooming all right, but the weeds were on the verge of taking over, and Erica frowned. If the lawn was being kept neatly mown, why were the gardens in such bad nick? Maybe the staff hadn't thought to hire a gardener as such, just someone to do the lawn, but even if it was just a matter of them not being able to identify weeds, they should still be able to see that the plants needed to be neatened up.

'It needs weeding,' she said.

'Yeah, I noticed that. Weird, isn't it? I guess maybe they haven't had time to organise a gardener since they opened. At least it's not blackberries or something really messy like that. Dandelions are kind of pretty.'

'Until there's a million of them.'

'So bring the whipper snipper round and offer to do their edges.'

Erica snorted. 'I could give them Johnno's phone number.' Johnno was the bloke who did the front lawn, going up and down alongside the driveway on his little ride-on mower. 'He might know someone who'd do it.'

The garden wasn't all that huge, so there was only so much admiring that Erica could do. As they walked back towards the building, she looked over at the people gathered around the tables. There were maybe twelve of them, but none of them a pale-faced girl with lank brown hair.

'Is that everyone?' she asked.

'Not quite,' Missy said. 'A few people went off with their families to have lunch, and there's an indoor rec room as well. I'll show you that too, and the dining room. The food's great here.'

'We had barbecue last night,' Erica said.

'We did too.' Missy pointed to the left of the door back into the house; there was a small paved area with a huge, new-looking black barbecue and Weber pot. 'It's supposed to be so that people can be in as normal a situation as possible, so they don't have fear reactions just to things being out of the ordinary as far as meals and stuff goes. That's why we all have our own rooms and bathrooms and don't have to share if we don't want to.'

'It sounds like they've thought of everything.'

'Pretty much. The only thing is that I think people get a little bored between sessions sometimes. I know that there's always a few people in the smokers' area.'

A second paved area was on the right of the door, and an older guy, maybe in his mid-thirties, was pacing back and forth, blowing clouds of blue-grey smoke into the air. There were two large ashtrays, the water-filled sort; Erica could only imagine how revolting they would be to clean out.

'Just don't you start smoking,' she said.

Missy rolled her eyes. 'As if. It's expensive and it makes you smell like that guy who's always on the town bus. I don't think he ever gets off and goes anywhere else. I think he just haunts that bus.' She held the door open for Erica. As they went inside, it started to rain, and suddenly Missy was holding the door for a mad rush of people. Erica stood out of the way and waited until they'd all gone past. Missy shut the door and grinned at her. 'Mad weather, huh? I'll give you the rest of the tour.'

The kitchen and dining area was one big open-plan space, with sleek modern everything, from the fridges and ovens built into their own spaces, to the neat lines of tables and chairs. There were more tables and chairs than Erica thought were necessary, since the clinic only catered for a maximum of twenty clients at a time, but maybe the staff ate with them, or there was room for families visiting at lunchtime. There were aproned staff members already in the kitchen preparing lunch— a vast array of sandwiches sat on coloured plastic trays, and as Erica watched, one of the cooks opened a fridge and started bringing out what seemed like an endless series of jugs of cordial.

'It's like school camp,' she commented.

'The food's better. I had a Milo last night that actually had milk in it. Maybe if they don't make as much of a profit as they're expecting they'll cut back, but I think they'd been doing pretty well.'

'Everything's so nice and new.'

'Yeah, well, maybe when it's been around longer than half a year it won't be.'

'You won't need to worry about it, you'll be cured by then.'

'Come on and I'll show you the rec room.'

Erica was expecting the rec room at least to be mundane, but she was surprised; a wide-screen television dominated one wall, while a second wall was lined with books, and the wall opposite that was glass, with a sliding door that led out to the smoking area. Another door marked STAFF ONLY was set into the wall with the bookshelves. The furniture here was the same pale blue as the employee uniforms and the bedsheets, a thankful departure from the cream theme of the reception area. There was a pay phone in one corner, and that was the only thing that stopped the room from looking like someone's living room.

'How do you decide what to watch?' she asked.

'I haven't really been out here much yet, but I guess people just have to be careful that they pick stuff that won't trigger anyone. It cuts out most of the news and that sort of thing. There're DVDs in the cupboard under the TV, but they're all pretty boring.'

'God, you really do have to be careful about everything you do, don't you? You never know whose toes you might be stepping on.'

'Yeah. Plus, they were supposed to be getting me a nightlight, but whoever was supposed to buy it forgot, so I had to sleep with the light in the bathroom on last night, and every time I so much as say hi to a staff member, they're falling over themselves to apologise, and I know that someone got sent out to buy one this morning. They're trying really hard to make sure that we're as comfortable as possible, and then they're turning around and trying to scare the crap out of us so they can figure out what's making us react the way we do.'

'They seem nice enough, though.'

'Oh, sure. Well, Doctor Morley's kind of creepy, but Doctor Chapman's amazing, and the rest of the staff are always so good. The patients are all pretty friendly too.'

'Who's the girl with the brown hair?' Erica gestured to indicate hair coming down to just below her chin.

Missy gave her another odd look. 'There isn't one.'

'Oh. I thought I saw her yesterday.'

'Must've been someone's sister visiting,' Missy said dismissively.

Must've been just a dream that didn't mean anything. Your subconscious saw the inside of one of those rooms and made up the rest. Get a grip.

The only reason the stupid dream was still hanging around in her head was because it was the first one she could remember having. That sort of dream, anyway. Usually she dreamed about surreal things like android wombats, or flying Mars Bar colonies, or picking out Scrabble tiles and seeing letters on them from Dr. Seuss's *On Beyond Zebra*. But in spite of her steady diet of horror novels, horror movies, and horror TV shows, she couldn't remember ever having had a nightmare that was based around any of them.

Erica didn't stay at the clinic much longer; lunchtime was announced and she decided to leave Missy to it. For her part, Missy didn't seem to mind, hugging her goodbye before going into the dining room, leaving Erica to make her own way out.

She paid closer attention to the doors as she walked down the hallway. Some were open, others closed; maybe Missy was right and she'd seen through an open one on her way out the day before, but the first bedroom was some distance from the front entrance. The door to room eight was closed, and though Erica tried the handle after a quick glance around to ascertain that nobody was watching, it was also locked. Good. Fine. She was being paranoid.

Erica waved to Cynthia on her way and hurried out to her car through the rain. Now that she was paying attention, the flower beds at the front of the clinic also looked bedraggled. Still, it wasn't her job to tell them how to run the place. She started the car and drove back down the long driveway and out onto the road. Maybe she should've stayed for lunch. Her tummy was rumbling. The chicken shop that Missy worked at was on her way home, though, and thinking of it made her suddenly crave their chips.

Despite eating chips and singing along with the radio the rest of the way home, Erica was focused on her driving. Which was how, when the girl stepped out of the trees and onto the road, she was able to brake in time and come to a messy stop, missing her by inches.

'*Shit!*' The girl was just standing there and staring at her. Erica shut the engine off and checked that the coast was clear.

When she turned back, however, the girl had gone.

Instead of opening the door, as planned, Erica lowered her head onto the top of the steering wheel. She was clearly going as nuts as Missy, and would be the next candidate for treatment at the Fear Clinic. Yeah, for sure, just as soon as they opened room eight back up again.

She was just thinking too goddamn much, that was the problem.

Either that or she was just being a dick.

Erica leaned back in her seat, pulled the paper off her chicken wrap, and ate it slowly, letting the sharp peppery taste of the sauce and the squidgy slide of the lettuce and the crunch of the coating on the chicken bring her back to the real world. When she was done she stuffed the wrapper into the plastic bag on the passenger side seat, restarted the car, and got on with the business of driving home.

There were no odd dreams that night.

50

Chapter Four

The following week passed with astonishing rapidity. Their parents managed to fit in a visit to Missy on Wednesday afternoon, but Kara, the girl who Erica had been planning to ask to cover for her one day so she could go visit Missy, came down with glandular fever and couldn't even get out of bed.

'I miss you, possum.' Talking on the phone just wasn't the same, but since their parents hadn't said much about Missy than that she looked like she was doing reasonably well, Erica needed to check in.

'Yeah, I miss you too. Nobody here blares their music through the halls the same way you do.' Missy laughed; it sounded forced, but it might have just been the poor quality connection.

'Have you been sleeping okay?'

'Last night was the worst; they woke me up every time I hit REM sleep and quizzed me about what I was dreaming.'

Erica snickered. 'I did that as a psych test subject that one time, remember?'

'Yeah, except instead of getting paid for my time, they're charging me for theirs.'

The plan for Saturday was to find out if Missy was coming home yet, or whether she felt that she needed longer. The staff of the Fear Clinic placed an emphasis on the client's decision when determining the length of the treatment course; if the clients felt well enough to go home, then they could go home. It was in the brochure. There was no minimum or maximum stay time, the brochure added, although the recommended minimum was two weeks, and the maximum anyone had stayed to date was two months. Their father had told Missy she could stay as long as she felt she needed. Erica was prepared to pull money out of her own savings if need be, as long as Missy came home capable of sleeping through the night.

Erica went downstairs Saturday morning to scramble some eggs for her parents, make them toast and coffee, and take the lot upstairs on a tray.

'Thank you, darling,' her mother said sleepily. 'Goodness, is that really the time?'

'I'd assume so,' Erica said. 'Daylight Savings was a fortnight ago.'

'Rick, wake up, it's nine-thirty.'

'Really?' Erica's father went from asleep to awake instantly. 'We've got to be there by ten-thirty!'

'Relax,' Erica said. 'We've got enough time for you to eat before we have to make a mad dash out of the door.'

She left them to it and went to get dressed.

The drive to Centralia was becoming very familiar. Erica looked out of the window and imagined the ground collapsing—if that field of cows just there suddenly vanished without warning, falling into a crack in the ground that seethed with an unnatural red light, and then the crack started widening, coming for the road—she would probably still be sick of the endless stretch of empty road that lay between Lilywood and Centralia.

What was waiting at the end of the trip, however, wasn't quite so boring.

A different receptionist was manning the counter. Her nametag said JOCELYN. She greeted them with a smile, but had to wait for a round of introductions before she could buzz Missy's room. She didn't hand them visitor passes, but asked that they sit in the waiting area.

Missy came into the room two minutes later, accompanied by a woman wearing a pale blue staff polo shirt. 'Hi, everyone,' she said quietly, eyes downcast.

'Possum, what's wrong?' Erica got to her feet and put a hand under Missy's chin, lifting her head so that she could see Missy's eyes. They were dull, with purple smudges beneath them. She turned to the nurse. 'She hasn't been sleeping,' she accused.

'Miss Sayle, your sister has been experiencing some important breakthroughs in her treatment,' the nurse said. 'Doctor Chapman will explain further.'

Erica's mother was still looking at Missy's face, one hand raised to half-cover her mouth. Her father looked equally worried. Neither of them had seen Missy look so bad before. But then, they weren't usually first to Missy's room in the night. Erica was. Erica had seen Missy first thing after a nightmare.

This was that, only turned up to eleven.

Before either of her parents could speak, Erica did. 'She'd better.'

Missy gave her a weak smile. 'I'm fine. Really,' she said. 'I think it's helping.'

'You don't look like it's helping,' said Erica.

'Good morning,' Doctor Chapman said, coming through the door marked PRIVATE that was in one corner of the reception area. She held the door open. 'If you'd like to come through to my office?'

Erica marched through and down the short hall into the doctor's office, which was where Missy's preliminary assessment had been held a month earlier. It at least looked like a real office instead of an example of how many household items could be found in cream or pale blue. There was even a fern in a basket hanging from the ceiling in one corner. Erica sat down and folded her hands in her lap, looking straight ahead. She had seen Missy looking tired and even downright exhausted before, but she had never seen that dull, dead expression. Ever. She wanted to know what could do that to a person, and she wanted to know *now*.

She had to wait, though. Doctor Chapman had medical charts showing Missy's vital signs for every evening and every morning. She also had a photo of Missy sacked out on one of the couches in the rec room; there was even a little smile on her face. The doctor had a vocabulary full of jargon, but it all boiled down to one thing for Erica: they were making Missy worse, not better. The charts and photos and words meant nothing. The look in Missy's eyes meant everything. The way that she kept glancing nervously at Doctor Chapman.

Finally, when Erica could stand it no longer, she asked, 'So how come she's not getting any better?'

Doctor Chapman gave her a politely confused look. 'I'm sorry?'

'*Look* at her!' Erica said. 'She looks like she hasn't slept all week, and like someone's been jumping out of her bathroom wearing a scary mask every night.'

'I'm *fine*,' Missy insisted, casting another nervous look at the doctor.

'The nature of the treatments can be exhausting at times. Last night's session was particularly intense. Melissa didn't get as much sleep as she has on other nights. But the treatments *are* working, and this chart showing her uninterrupted sleep periods backs that up.' Doctor Chapman tapped one of the papers, and Erica reluctantly leaned over and looked at it. The chart showed that Missy was sleeping longer and longer each night before waking up, and going back to sleep within minutes. A couple of the nights were marked NO INTERVENTION NEEDED.

'What's that mean?' Erica pointed to the capitalised words.

'Only that Melissa went back to sleep of her own accord, rather than one of the nurses needing to attend her to reassure her.'

'Reassure—'

Finally her father spoke up. 'Erica, go wait in reception, please. Your mother and I will ask the rest of the questions.' He looked thundery; she was going to cop it when they were on the way home.

'But—'

'*Go.*'

Erica went. Her tummy was starting to rumble, so she filched one of the chocolate biscuits off the coffee table when she got out to reception, and sat in a corner eating it. Jocelyn gave her a funny look from behind the counter, but didn't say anything. Wise woman.

She only had to wait half an hour, though she'd expected it to take longer. Missy came out first, still looking wan but smiling; their parents followed her; and Doctor Chapman brought up the rear, with a facial expression that was not quite a smile, but edging into the territory of being a gleeful smirk.

'I'm going to give another week a shot,' Missy said, before Erica could say anything. 'I think I'm really close to being able to sleep right through the night. I mean, here I am in a strange place, and yet I'm still sleeping almost all night without worrying about what might be in the bathroom. If I can do it here, I'm sure I can do it at home.'

Erica said nothing, but got up and hugged Missy tightly. 'You're right,' she said. 'Those charts show you're getting a lot more sleep than at home, and I'm sorry I was being so silly about it.' She let Missy go and turned to her parents. 'Mum, Dad, Doctor Chapman, I'm so sorry. I overreacted.'

She'd been thinking pretty hard for the past half hour and concluded that the dream was just a dream.

As for the girl on the road, that was just her mind making stuff up because she watched too damn many horror movies. In fact, she was certain that if she went home and looked through her DVD covers or checked out a few of the actors on IMDb, she'd find the girl with the pale face and brown hair. It was all in her head, and the only reason that she was overreacting so much was because she simply wasn't used to horror movies having any sort of negative effect on her thought processes, when they evidently *had* gotten to her after all; it had just taken a while, and that was all there was to it.

Her mother smiled at her; her father looked mollified, although she suspected she was still in for a bit of an earbashing on the drive home. 'I'm glad you've changed your mind,' her mother said, reaching out and patting her on the shoulder. Doctor Chapman just smiled and nodded, as if she saw such squabbles all the time. And hey, if every patient came out looking as wrecked as Missy did, she probably got a lot of negative reactions from their families.

'Do you want us to come by again tomorrow, Missy?' their father asked.

Missy shook her head. 'Maybe during the week, if you can make it.'

'I did bring you some more clean clothes, Missy. They're out in the car. I'll just go get them.'

'That's a coincidence, 'cause I've got some dirty ones I can bring out.' Missy turned and moved towards her room. Erica followed her.

'What the hell was that all about?' Missy demanded as soon as they were alone. 'God, we're going to have to find a clinic for you next, except I don't know any around here that treat stupid!'

'I said I was sorry,' Erica said. 'Really. I *was* being stupid.'

'Sure. And you sounded about as sincere as a Barbie doll's boobs.' Missy picked up a plastic bag that was already half full of clothes and shovelled a few more bits and pieces into it. 'What gives?'

'Nothing! I'm just—I don't know, possum, I guess I'm just worried for you, and stressing out about having a crappy job, and it's making my mind do some weird stuff. I'll be okay. You'll be okay. Dad's wallet might be a bit thinner for a while, but he'll get over it, and life will go on.'

Missy knotted the top of the bag. 'You're gonna have to stop calling me "possum" soon, you know. I won't be twitchy any more.'

Erica grinned. 'Sure thing, jellybean.'

Missy groaned and threw the clothes bag at her; Erica caught it with ease. 'Jellybean doesn't count either!'

'Why not?' Erica asked. 'Jellybeans are about the least twitchy thing I can think of.'

'What's going on in here?' their mother asked from the doorway. 'I came back and you'd both vanished.'

'Just airing the dirty laundry, Mum,' Erica said, her grin spreading wider.

'You're very silly.'

'I know.'

The laundry exchange done, Erica and her parents said goodbye to Missy again and headed out to the car. Erica would've liked a longer visit, but her father had research to do, and her mother was working to complete their tax return—guiltily late, but as she often said, 'The shoemaker's children go barefoot.' To which her husband usually countered, 'Yes, but the shoemaker wasn't facing a failure to lodge penalty of hundreds of dollars for not replacing his kids' shoes,' a reply that might have been funny the first time but, like the line that prompted it, was now just old and tired and needed to be shot and put out of everyone else's misery.

Once they were on the road, Erica braced herself for the inevitable telling-off from her father, and was therefore more than a little surprised when it didn't come. He was quiet as usual, probably thinking about the case that he was prosecuting, and said nothing after asking her mother what radio station she wanted to listen to. It was unnerving, but Erica didn't dare open her mouth, in case he was just waiting for her to say one more stupid thing.

She caught herself looking out of the window when they got to the place where the girl had walked out in front of her car, but of course there was nothing there.

CHAPTER FIVE

Erica went up to her room when they got home, after taking Missy's stuff into the laundry and starting a load—easy enough, since practically all Missy wore was dark colours. She was starting to worry about how messy things were getting, as her bookshelves were overflowing and she wasn't entirely sure that everything would fit back on even if it were put in neatly and the right way up, instead of just being shoved in any old how.

She started by completely emptying the shelves, piling the books on her bed, and sorting them by author. Then she put them back, squeezing them up as much as possible—at least most of them were cheap second-hand paperbacks she'd found at various op shops, rather than hardcover copies; she had always been capable of waiting for the paperback release or, in particularly important cases (*Lisey's Story* came to mind, although she had been a bit disappointed by that one—it wasn't as horror-y as some of King's other books), going on the hold list at the local library. And even that was a big deal, because the closest branch was in Centralia.

Once that was done, she hung up her clean, ironed clothes, picked several pieces of magnetic poetry out of the carpet and put them back on her whiteboard, and then sat down at her computer to do some practice house hunting. Her parents had warned her repeatedly to watch out for hidden expenses, and as a result she had set her maximum price as low as possible. It kept creeping up as the balance in her savings account increased, but with the way the interest rates kept rising, she was going to have to get a pretty damn spectacular job if she wanted to be able to pay her mortgage and still have fun, exciting things like be able to eat three meals a day and have hot showers.

When her mobile rang, she grabbed it straight away, grateful for anything that gave her an excuse to turn away from the highly desirable properties that nonetheless would cost her far more than she could afford to spend. The caller display said it was Toby.

'Hey, you. What's up?'

'I've got writer's block.'

'Do you want me to come over there?' Erica asked.

'No, that's all right, you needn't bother yourself. Just make sure there's some afternoon tea ready when I get to your house.'

Erica snickered. 'You're so presumptuous.'

'I'm in a corn chips and salsa mood. See you soon.'

Erica looked at the clock on the computer and realised it was already two in the afternoon, and moreover that she'd forgotten to have any lunch, and hurried down to the kitchen. She made herself a Vegemite sandwich and pulled a bag of Doritos and a jar of salsa out of the pantry, setting them out on the coffee table in the living room. She got the Scrabble set out and set it up, and then went back into the kitchen to get each of them a Pepsi can out of the fridge.

It was reassuring to be at home and doing such mundane tasks after seeing what the Fear Clinic was like. It was so *sterile*. Maybe if it had been eighty years old with three storeys and an attic and creaky stairs and weird paintings on the walls and staff who were a bit sinister, she would feel more comfortable about the place, like it lived up to its name.

Toby arrived ten minutes later, wandering up the side path and straight into the living room. He claimed that the formal lounge room and dining room at the front of the house gave him hives. Erica doubted that very much, since his only real allergy was to peanuts, but she put up with it just in case one day someone broke in and replaced the leather sofas with peanut butter sandwiches—this being Toby's idea of a crisis situation. How he'd gotten a job as a serious journalist she didn't know, since his talents were pretty clearly more suited to making up total and utter nonsense.

'So how's Missy doing?' Toby asked once they were both settled down, facing each other across the Scrabble board.

'Fine.' Erica shook the bag of tiles. 'I thought she looked pretty wrecked, but she said she was doing okay.'

'It's about time something worked for her.'

Erica rolled her eyes. 'God, tell me about it. I'm tempted to wake her up at three in the morning on her first night back, just to show her how it feels.'

'I think she's probably more than aware of how it feels.'

'I know, I know.' Erica drew her tiles and passed Toby the bag. 'But, you know, I can't help it. She's not the only one who gets affected by her damn nightmares. I've been going nuts this past week.'

'You were already nuts.'

'Be serious. I had a freaky dream, and I thought I saw this girl standing in the road.' Erica fidgeted with her tiles. She had a Q, which could be useful, but no U.

'Did she have a hook hand?'

'Just make your move, smartarse.'

Toby did so, beginning the game with CRAYON. They played for best out of three; it was a close-run thing, but Erica surprised herself by not getting completely trounced.

They had barely packed up the board when Toby said, 'Let's go for a drive.'

'Where to?'

'Duncan's Creek.'

'Toby, that's over an hour away.'

'It's perfect weather for a barbecue, and the park doesn't close until eight. We can get there, wander around for a while, eat, and then head home. Please? We can even take my car so yours doesn't get all muddy crossing the ford.'

'All right,' Erica said. 'Let me tell Mum and pack some food.'

Her mother was pounding away at her computer when Erica tapped at her study door, but turned around and smiled right away. 'Hi, honey. What's up?'

'Toby and I are going to go for a drive and a picnic tea,' Erica said. 'If that's okay.'

'Of course it is! Where were you planning to go?'

'Just up to Duncan's Creek,' Erica said. 'Don't worry, if we're in a horrible accident on the way I'll call you and let you know. I've got my mobile.'

Her mother groaned. 'Please try not to be.'

'Sure.' Erica crossed the room, bent, and kissed her mother on the cheek. 'We'll be back by nine-thirty, maybe ten, okay?'

'That's fine. If you get stuck in that swamp, ring me *before* you ring the towing company, okay? That way I can at least come and meet you in case they can't give you a ride home.'

'We're taking Toby's car. It'll plough through anything.'

'It looks like it *has.*'

Erica laughed. 'True, that.'

'Don't disturb your father on the way out. He's very busy at the moment.'

'Okay.'

They finally got rolling at three-thirty, not putting the radio on because Erica had a moral objection to bringing work home with her, not to mention that there was always too much to talk about. To begin with, Toby wanted more details on Missy's treatment.

'There's not really that much more to tell,' Erica said. 'They're quite closemouthed about what they do.'

'But it involves some sort of simulation, doesn't it? Virtual reality?'

'Yes. Only the brochure made it sound less technological. I thought they were just going to make her sleep with the lights off for a week and see what happened, but apparently there are tests and a program and—oh, I don't know. I haven't seen inside the treatment room because they lock the doors, and I barely got to speak to Missy last visit.'

'How come?'

Erica told him why, briefly, feeling more than a little embarrassed about how silly she'd been. She mentioned the bad dream that she'd had, and the girl who had stepped out in front of her car. Toby kept his eyes on the road, but nodded every so often, or made encouraging 'mmmm-hmmm' noises.

'What about texting her? She might not have time for long calls, but she can probably text.'

'I will. Right now.' Erica pulled out her phone and typed a message, and then tried to send it. 'Damn. No reception. I'll do it when we get back home.' Reception was notoriously patchy in and around Lilywood and Centralia; the lack of mobile phone towers explained it, but nobody ever explained why there *was* a lack of mobile phone towers. Presumably the phone companies were too busy engaged in upselling cable internet packages to their existing customers.

It was a nice afternoon; warm, but not overly hot, and the sky was completely clear and blue and beautiful.

'Days like today were the best in primary school,' Erica said. 'I used to lie on my back and stare up at the sky and think it was like a big blue bowl turned upside down over the world.'

'And then you imagined vampire bats attacking the students.'

'Maybe,' Erica admitted. 'Maybe just a couple of the other kids who weren't very nice to me.'

'I just used to imagine a dragon swooping down and incinerating all the bullies.'

'At least mine was possible.'

'Around here? I think vampire bats are less likely than dragons in these parts.'

'You never know.'

'Can you remind me when we're getting close to the turnoff? I've forgotten how far up it is.'

Splashing through the ford and then starting the barbecue was enough of a distraction to keep the two of them busy for a little while, but Toby resumed his role as her self-appointed therapist.

'So, have you got any idea why you're stressing out at the moment?' he asked, pricking the sausages with a fork.

'I think it's just work—the travelling and the boredom, mainly—and worrying about Missy,'

'Are you still job hunting?'

'Yeah, but I need to move somewhere bigger before I can get a better job. I've set my sights slightly higher than community radio.'

'You know, if you'd started there straight out of high school, you could be station manager by now.'

'Oh, shut up. Just because I'm not planning to spend my entire life in one town ...'

'I'm sure you'll get where you want to go soon enough, Erica. But right now, enjoy the fresh air and the smell of dinner and live for this moment, not for what you might be able to do in a year's time. And when you get home, try to keep living for the day you're in, not jumping ahead all the time. I'm surprised you're not the one having nightmares—except for that one from the other night, and *one* hardly counts, especially not when you stack it up against all the years of bad dreams Missy has had.'

'Thank you, Toby. I'm pretty sure that's a nicer version of the lecture Dad nearly gave me earlier today.'

Toby poked the sausages and just smiled at her. 'Lots of other people are stress-bunnies too. You don't have to be one.'

'I'm not a stress-bunny, I just want to do something with my life. And why *bunny*? So far as I can tell, bunnies are about the least stressed animals around, except maybe that really big old tortoise at the zoo.'

'The bunnies in *Watership Down* got pretty stressed sometimes.'

Erica shook her head. 'Come on, Toby, you know I've never read that.'

'You should. It's got some scenes you'd really enjoy. Ritual mutilation, stalking, pure suspense as the rabbits wait to see if the enemy rabbits are going to break into the warren and kill them all ... you'd love it.'

'I think we have different ideas of what constitutes horror.'

'You don't think ritual mutilation constitutes horror?'

'Sure it does. But not when it's being performed by *bunnies*.'

'One of these days I will sit you down and tie you up and read *Harry Potter and the Philosopher's Stone* to you,' Toby said, flipping the sausages one by one, 'and you will become enraptured by the tale of an orphan boy who discovers he is a wizard and grows up to save the world from evil.'

'No.'

'There're ghosts.'

'No.'

'Necromancy?'

'Sure, fine, whatever. Hey, you know what? I'll borrow the DVD sometime.'

'You,' said Toby, 'with your attitude, are singlehandedly responsible for the illiteracy rate amongst young students. They hear opinions like yours and decide, oh, hey, if that grown-up thinks reading is stupid, then it must be stupid.'

'I happen to own three hundred and forty-two books,' Erica said. 'I *love* reading. I just don't like reading unrealistic stuff.'

'Because a rabid dog bailing two people up in a car is realistic? Because a teenage girl with telekinesis going ballistic is realistic? Because some crazy lady kidnapping a writer and holding him prisoner is realistic?'

'Yes.'

Toby let out a great dramatic sigh and almost slapped his forehead with his hand, remembering that he was still holding the tongs just in time to avoid poking his eye out. 'Young people these days just don't appreciate the value of a good fantasy world.'

'That's because crap like that *Eragon* gets published.'

'It's not my fault you picked one of the worst books on the face of the planet to commence your foray into fantasy literature with. You should have sought my advice, young lady. I'd've soon set you on the right path.'

'Kids' books with trains and schoolkids on the front and sparkly stars in the border? Sorry. Give me *Pet Sematary* any time. That was an uplifting kids' book.'

'Didn't the kid get run over?'

'Mostly.'

Toby winced. 'At least if a dragon attacks you, you either escape or get fried. You don't get "mostly eaten".'

Erica smirked. 'Maybe if you had a dragon who was like a spider and could spin webs and hang its victims up to eat later, you would.'

Toby looked pained. 'Now I'm imagining the bastard offspring of Shelob and Smaug and really wishing I hadn't.' He caught the quizzical expression on Erica's face. 'Giant spider and dragon, both from the *Lord of the Rings* world.' He picked up a plate and piled the sausages onto it. 'I hope you're hungry.'

Erica put two pieces of bread on her plate and squirted tomato sauce onto each of them, sprinkled a little bit of shredded cheese on top, and laid a sausage diagonally across each one. 'I could eat a million of these,' she said.

'I would have nightmares for months if I had to watch you do it. Pass the sauce please.' Toby made his own sausages in bread look like roadkill with lavish amounts of tomato sauce. 'I'd love a Pepsi, thanks for offering.'

Erica passed one over. 'You're a mercenary scumbag.'

'That's Thursday nights. Saturday nights I'm a neutral good wizard with a leather cape, but we're taking a week off because the GM has to hand in his thesis.'

Erica blinked. 'Sorry, I think you stopped speaking English there.'

'Dungeons and Dragons,' Toby explained. 'Roleplaying. Gaming. Dice.'

'Oh, that.'

'I did offer to lend you *Baldur's Gate* to play on the computer so you'd understand,' Toby said sadly. 'Your exact response was, "Is it harder than Minesweeper?".'

'Hey, I played *The 7th Guest* when I was in primary school,' Erica protested. 'I'm not completely game-illiterate.'

'That was over ten years ago, so yes, actually, you *are* completely game-illiterate. Remind me to break out *Betrayal at House on the Hill* when you come over next. Missy won't like it, but Aaron loves it, and you will too. It's a board game and it's got horror elements, *really* horror elements, not just ghosts and necromancy, although those are in it too. It's really tense, especially if you play with low lights and some creepy music playing.'

'Creepy music I can provide,' Erica said. 'I have the *Silent Hill* soundtrack, *House on Haunted Hill*, *Saw* ...'

Toby grinned. 'I'm not surprised.'

They fell silent for a few minutes as they ate. The noises of the bush seemed louder than ever as the day drew to a close; early-rising nocturnal creatures added their voices to the goodnight cries of those animals who only ventured out during the sunlit hours. The water rushing over the weir sounded so strong and so eternal that it was impossible to believe there would ever be a shortage of it. A cool breeze started to blow, fanning the flames of the fire inside the barbecue, and bringing the mingled smells of pine and eucalyptus through the picnic area.

'I wish we could camp up here,' Toby said, popping the last bite of his sausage into his mouth. 'We'd see so many animals at night.'

'We'd get torn to shreds by a homicidal maniac with hooks for hands who escaped from the local asylum,' Erica said.

'Well, considering that the Fear Clinic is probably the nearest psychiatric facility of any sort, we'll probably be okay. We'd just need to arm ourselves with a bunch of spiders and mice and clowns.'

'Clowns?'

'Coulrophobia happens to be quite common, I'll have you know. Clowns are freaky. You can't see their real faces and they could be up to anything behind all that white greasepaint.' Toby shivered.

'Can't sleep, clown will eat me?'

'Exactly.'

Erica thought of Pennywise; thought of the clown puppet from *Saw*. 'I can see where you're coming from.'

'Good.'

'Are *you* afraid of clowns?'

Toby looked uncomfortable. 'Not really. Not normally. I mean, I'm not gonna freak out if I go to a circus, or to the Show, or something like that. But I'm never going to be a big fan.'

'I never knew that. How come you never told me?'

'I thought you'd think it was funny.'

'Come on, Toby, don't be silly.'

'Silly? You call your sister "possum" because she's so jumpy. I thought you'd start calling me … I don't know, something like that.'

'The best I can come up with on short notice is "scaredy-cat" actually.'

'That's a relief.'

'Give me a week, I'll have something else for you.'

But she didn't have a week.

Chapter Six

Someone was shining a light in her eyes. A little light, like a red laser pointer. Erica groaned, threw her arm across her face, and wriggled to an upright position, and then peeked cautiously out from underneath her arm.

The red spot danced across her bookshelves, across her *X-Files* movie poster, coming to rest on one of the few bare patches of wall, just above her computer monitor. It jiggled a little, and then changed into the words HELP ME.

'Not again.'

HELP ME.

'Look, I know I'm just lucid dreaming. My stupid subconscious got that from "Paper Hearts", and I'm going back to sleep now.' Erica sprawled out comfortably and stuck her head under the pillow.

Thirty seconds later, she was staring at the wall again.

HELP ME.

'Who are you?' Erica asked in a whisper.

ROSE.

'I'm being talked to by a plant?'

MY NAME IS ROSE. HELP ME.

This was getting just a little too complicated for the middle of the night. 'Help you *how*? Who are you?'

I DIED AT THE FEAR CLINIC.

Erica froze, hands clutching the bedspread. 'You *died*?'

THEY HAVE TO BE STOPPED.

'But how did you die? What happened?'

The light flickered, hesitant, and then merely repeated, THEY HAVE TO BE STOPPED. Then it vanished.

Erica curled up into a ball, snuggling down under the covers, and waited to wake up.

The first thing that she did the next morning was to go over to the wall and look at it, but of course there was no sign that anything had been there, and why would there be? Even if it hadn't been a dream, laser pointers didn't leave a mark. Moreover, laser pointers didn't magically change from a single dot to a series of words, at least not in her experience.

On a whim, she booted up her computer and brought up the homepage of the local newspaper, then initiated a search through the last six months of obituaries for anyone named Rose. Given that there were two nursing homes in Lilywood, she was expecting quite a few hits. She left the search running while she went downstairs to get breakfast. The only reason she was bothering with even looking was because the information was available online, thanks to Toby, who had done a lot of work getting the archives up and running and had then proceeded to hand the job off to someone else to continue updating it as soon as he got bored.

She made raisin toast for breakfast and ate it standing over the sink, too fidgety to sit down just yet.

When Erica got back upstairs, the search was complete. As she'd suspected, there was a list of about twenty hits. Still, that wasn't too many to go through. She sat down, sipping her Milo, and scanned through them. None of them stood out as particularly unusual—most of them related to Rose Williams, who had passed away in her sleep—until the seventh one:

> BUTLER, Paul Anthony (43); BUTLER, Michelle Therese (nee McGuire) (44); BUTLER, Rose Sarah (18); BUTLER, Melanie Leanne (15). Passed away on the 28th of October following a tragic car accident near Centralia. They will be greatly missed by all those whom their lives touched. Family and friends are invited to attend the funeral services, which will be held at Lilywood Funeral Home on the 2nd of November at 11 AM.

Erica clicked the back button and did a search for BUTLER. They had been from Centralia; pillars of the community, it seemed, judging by the number of notices. There was a short article talking about Michelle's work on the fundraising committee of Centralia High School, about Melanie's dazzling academic career tragically cut short by her untimely death, about Paul's tireless contribution to the community effort of rebuilding Centralia Primary School after it had burned down, and about how sad it was that Rose had died just after her crippling claustrophobia had been cured by the Centralia Fear Clinic.

'No way,' Erica whispered, staring at the monitor.

Her whiteboard rattled on the wall. She turned around so fast to look at it that she nearly gave herself whiplash.

The magnetic poetry was moving, one word at a time sliding down the board to the blank space at the bottom.

> YOU SCREAM BUT NOT DREAM
> TV IS DEATH
> TIME IS VOID
> PLEASE

'What ...' She clung to the arms of her chair, knuckles turning white.

All of the tiles abruptly fell off the board onto the carpet, pattering like rain.

'No, no, no.' Erica squeezed her eyes tight shut. 'Still dreaming. Not real.'

When she next opened her eyes, the clock read 11.30 AM and her head ached from oversleeping, but the poetry hadn't moved, the computer monitor was dark, and her Milo cup was gone. She got up and went downstairs. There was a note from her mother on the kitchen bench.

> Dear Erica,
>
> We've gone antique shopping for a few hours. Leaving at 10.30, should be back by 2.30, but will call if we're running any later. We didn't wake you since we know how much you <u>love</u> antiques.
>
> Love, Mum

Erica grinned, tossed the note into the recycling bin, and went back upstairs to change into her bathers. She occasionally got nervous about swimming alone, but if she just did some quiet laps, she would be fine. It was definitely more than an hour since she'd eaten her raisin toast, after all.

But that was a dream ... wasn't it? If I was dreaming that part, why am I not hungry now?

She bumped the computer desk as she was pulling her nightie off over her head. When she emerged from the folds of cloth, the computer had woken up and she was confronted with the obituary search staring blandly back at her from the screen.

So I sleepwalked ...

But she'd never sleepwalked in her life. Ever. Missy did it—Missy even sleep *ran* sometimes, crying, her feet thumping along the hallway until Erica caught her and steered her back to her room—but Erica always slept the night through undisturbed unless Missy woke her.

Erica finished putting her bathers on, because standing there naked staring at the computer wasn't going to get her anywhere, and went downstairs. On her way through the kitchen she checked the dish rack. Her raisin toast plate was in it, and so was her Milo mug, both washed, along with dishes that must have been from her parents' breakfast. She added this little fact to the pile already in her brain. It would help if someone invented a way to get thoughts out of her brain and look at them in order, instead of having them all churning around in there like laundry tumbling in the dryer. So far all she had was fluff and lint.

Without really thinking about what she was doing, she pulled the Scrabble tiles out of the box and tipped them onto the coffee table, turning them all right side up, leaving them there as an invitation. Then she went out to the pool, walking slowly down the steps instead of making her usual splashing entrance via the diving platform.

She swam a few laps, concentrating on style rather than speed, letting her thoughts run to the next level down from where she was thinking about keeping her legs straight and arms moving smoothly. She put her face under the water instead of holding her head awkwardly up, as if she were dogpaddling instead of freestyling.

Mum could have come and got the Milo cup and washed it. Then that means that part was real. Including the magnetic poetry moving. And that's just not possible. I don't believe that the red light dream was real, but if that wasn't real, why did I do the obituary search in the first place? Chasing a dream? That's insane. So maybe it was all a dream. But if that's true, then how come my Milo mug and my plate were in the drainer? Unless they weren't mine. Maybe Dad had two coffees and just grabbed a fresh mug instead of refilling his first one. But he never does that, and besides, nobody uses my X-Files mug without asking. On the other hand, it did get washed.

But even so, that doesn't explain why the computer was on and I'd looked that page up. How can the red light have existed at all? She was only moving little things around before, not actually making something appear where it wasn't. That poor girl. I can't imagine being claustrophobic. I wonder what that part about TV being death meant? Unless she didn't mean TV, but was limited by the available words. I hate when that happens.

If Rose died in a car accident, how come she's trying to warn me about the Fear Clinic? Why couldn't she tell me more with the red light instead of being so frigging cryptic?

Erica flipped over, changing smoothly to backstroke. The medley relay had been her favourite event at the school swimming carnival, although the school pool wasn't as nice and warm as this one was. On her back, she could see how blue the sky was, completely clear of any clouds. She should probably call Toby anyway and see if he wanted to swim. Then she could call the Fear Clinic and find out what their story was about Rose Butler.

Sure. And then you can grab the Yellow Pages and look up a therapist who can explain to you exactly why all of this is crazy. You need to get a grip! It's got to all be a dream, the red light, the magnetic poetry, all of it. Have some real breakfast and wake up to yourself.

Erica climbed out of the pool and went inside to call Toby, and saw that the Scrabble tiles had moved.

PLEASE BELIEVE

Despite having hoped for something to happen, it was still hard not to scream.

She drew in a long, deep breath, let it out slowly. Again and again, in through the nose, out through the mouth. Inhale for four, hold for four, exhale for four. Missy called it 'breathing in triangles' and did it even though she didn't think it helped her anxiety much.

It helped Erica. Focusing on her breathing helped her push away the sound of her heart thumping in her ears. The rest of the world had gone utterly silent; she breathed until sound came back in the form of birdsong and traffic. She breathed and rubbed her arms until the goosebumps went away.

Then she picked up the phone, speed-dialling Toby and listening to it ring and ring and ring.

'Hi, Erkel,' Toby answered eventually.

'Oh for God's sake. Can you come over? We need to talk.'

'I can't believe you're breaking up with me.'

'Toby! Be serious. I might have had more weird dreams last night.'

'*Might* have had? I'll be there in half an hour. I need to shave, I look like I'm wearing an echidna.'

'Don't worry about that, okay? Just come over. I'll be in the living room.' Erica hung up and sat down on the couch. This was it. Either Toby would come over and see the tiles and hear about her dreams and have a solution for her, or he would ask to use her phone so that he could ring the psych ward and have her committed.

When Toby arrived, she was pacing from the living room to the kitchen and back again, occasionally sipping at a can of Pepsi, but already very wired. She'd changed into a sleeveless top and a long skirt, but still felt as if she was being constricted somehow. Toby slid the back door open and stepped inside, giving her a worried look.

'Sit down and tell me what's going on.'

Erica sat down and gestured to the Scrabble tiles. 'I didn't write that.'

Toby bent over the table. 'Please believe what?'

'I had these dreams. Maybe. They might not have been dreams. I dreamed that I woke up in the middle of the night and there was a red light writing words on the wall. Then I dreamed that I woke up and my magnetic poetry said things and I searched on the Internet to find the name from the red light dream and I found her. The paper said she died in a car accident, but she says she died at the Fear Clinic and

I'm scared for Missy, but I don't know if I should be or if it was all just a dream.'

Toby looked at her, then down at the Scrabble tiles, then back at her. 'You didn't do this yourself?' His voice was asking a simple question; his cautious expression implied that he was glad that she didn't have any sharp objects immediately to hand.

Then the Scrabble tiles began to move. They slid over the polished wooden surface of the coffee table slowly, as if whatever was pushing them was expending a tremendous amount of energy to do so.

HELP ME

'Oh hell no,' Toby breathed. 'What is *this*?'

Erica turned her left arm palm-up and pinched the soft white flesh of her forearm hard, digging in with her short nails. The pain was real and intense and awake. 'This is happening, Toby, this is real. How can this be happening?'

COME TO HOSPITAL

'What can we do, Rose?'

STOP THEM

'How?' Toby asked. 'How the hell can we—we don't even know what's going on!' He stared at Erica as the tiles kept moving. 'Erica, this *can't* be happening.'

STOP THE MACHINES

'The virtual reality machines ... is that how they killed you? Did they electrocute you or something?' Toby's voice mixed disbelief and fascination.

ACCIDENT

'Is it in their records?'

MAYBE

The tiles were moving even more slowly.

'Erica.' Toby tore his gaze away from the tiles and met her eyes. 'If this is a joke, or a trick ...'

'It's *real*.' Erica pinched him this time, and Toby pushed her hand away as the tiles slid into their last message.

WEAK

COME NOW

Erica jumped to her feet. 'We've got to go. Now. We can get in. It's visiting hours. I can get Missy out and maybe you can get into the offices behind reception and find their files.'

'We can't just break in there.'

'We have to. They're killing people.'

Toby sighed and got up. 'Come on. We'll go. Like you said, it's visiting hours. We can see Missy, talk to her, and you'll see it's all okay.'

He looked like he didn't believe her, didn't believe that it wasn't just her messing with him, and that *hurt*.

They took Toby's car as it was blocking Erica's in the driveway, which was just as well since Erica didn't think she could possibly drive. She had left a message for her parents, saying that she and Toby were going for a drive and would be back soon.

'Slow down,' Erica said, when they were approaching the place where she'd seen the girl in the road the last time. She looked out of the window as

Toby obediently slowed the car to a crawl. 'Stop. Stop here.' She opened the car door before the car had completely stopped, almost stumbled getting out, and then regained her feet, crossing the grass quickly to one of the trees that lined the roadside. It had a wooden cross bound to it and flowers that, though they were dead, looked relatively recent. BUTLER, the cross said. There was a tiny teddy bear tied to the cross as well.

Erica looked up and saw Rose step out from behind the tree. She wore a white long-sleeved shirt and a black skirt, black tights, and black boots. Her brown hair hung around her face and she had traces of makeup on that hadn't quite been removed. There were lines around her eyes as if she'd been wearing something over them. And she was completely transparent, fading in and out of existence.

'What the—what—' Toby stammered.

'Rose.' Erica stared at the ghost. Fear blurred the edges of her thoughts, but so did a kind of relief.

Toby could see Rose too.

Rose was real.

The flash of a digital camera turned Rose into a brilliantly glowing girl-shape for a moment.

'Stop that,' Erica said.

'But ...' Toby's voice shook. 'It's—she's real—I need proof—'

'No buts. Just quit it.' She returned her attention to Rose. 'We're going up there now. We're going to stop whatever's going on up there.' Now she could hear typing. 'Toby, what the hell are you doing?'

'Can you speak up? I can't quote you if I can't hear you.'

Rose's eyes lit up at the sight of Toby balancing his laptop on the hood of the car. She drifted over, half walking, half floating, and then vanished. Toby leapt back. Erica hurried to join him.

There were words appearing on the laptop's screen, and the keys were being pressed one by one, with great effort. Erica could only see the very tips of Rose's fingers, but they were more solid than before.

'Oh my God,' she whispered, as she read what was being written on the screen.

> they're doing more than just trying to treat us
> but i don't know what there is another level
> below what you see
>
> they make us afraid and then they take the fear

'How? How do they take the fear?'

> they use the machines the vr machines i don't
> know how it works
>
> please you have to stop them before more
> people die

'How did you really die, Rose?' Toby broke in.

> something went wrong in my brain and i
> collapsed

everything went dark and then i woke up but i
wasn't in my body anymore

and i'm not the only one two more people died

nathan and linh before i was there

Erica stared at Toby and Toby stared back, both of
them silent, shocked. It took them a long moment to
realise that Rose had gone.

'We have to get up there now,' Erica said.

'I agree. We've got to get Missy out of there and
then worry about exposing them.'

Erica opened the car door and got in. Toby took an
extra minute to save the file Rose had used to speak to
them and stow the laptop in its carry bag on the back
seat before getting back into the car and starting the
engine.

'How do you think we can tell people about what's
going on there?' he asked.

'I don't know. How can we? We can't very well go
public by saying that a ghost told us what was really
going on. We need proof.'

'Case files for Rose and the other two—Nathan and
Linh. Surely they'd have to have evidence that Rose
was dead before the car accident.'

'As if anyone keeps records like that. What if
someone went looking?' Erica couldn't keep the
sarcasm out of her voice despite the fact that it was
exactly the sort of thing that she needed.

'Have you got any better ideas?'

'Maybe there are other patients there who were around when Rose died. Paramedics who were at the car accident. Hey, maybe someone did an autopsy!'

Toby was shaking his head. 'I remember that one. They all burned in the car. There wasn't enough left to autopsy. They had to make the ID from dental records. There were about a million obits for them, and most of the people who were submitting one were asking us if it was actually true.'

They drove the rest of the way in silence. It was one o'clock by the time they pulled into the car park at the Fear Clinic. The building had once looked almost cheerful, filled as it was with the promise of a cure for Missy. Now the windows looked like blank staring eyes, and as they walked through the front door, Erica shivered.

They went straight to Missy's room.

She wasn't there.

'Don't panic yet,' Toby said, catching Erica's hand as she knotted it into a fist. 'She could be in another room or in the garden.'

Erica led the way down the corridor to the back door. She looked into the garden and saw people sitting around the tables, but Missy wasn't amongst them.

She glanced into the rec room, but Missy wasn't there either, though a few of the patients were watching *Bananas in Pyjamas*.

'Bad news for anyone with a fruit phobia,' Toby whispered, and Erica had to stifle a burst of hysterical giggling. They went back the other way, through to the open-plan kitchen and dining room, and Missy was there, sitting at one of the long tables, eating a sandwich. She had a glass of orange juice in front of her, along with the newspaper, and she was doing a crossword.

'Missy!' Erica hurried forward, and then slowed down as she realised that Doctor Chapman was sitting at the next table along with her own lunch. 'Hi,' she said. 'Surprise!'

'What're you doing here?'

'Um, we brought you a present because you're recovering so well. It's in your room. Come and see!'

'Can I finish my lunch first? It's the best chicken salad sandwich I've ever had.'

'Better than mine?' Erica forced a laugh. 'I don't believe you.'

Missy took another huge mouthful, chewed, swallowed. 'Try a bite.'

Erica tore a corner off. Despite her anxiety, she had to admit that the sandwich really was very good. Out of the corner of her eye she saw Doctor Chapman get up and leave the room, and she leaned in close to her sister. 'We've got to get you out of here.'

'What?'

'Bring your sandwich. We'll get your stuff and go.'

'You're nuts.'

'No. Seriously. We have to leave.'

'People have died here, Missy,' Toby put in. 'We're afraid you'll be next.'

Missy ate another bit of her sandwich and washed it down with the juice. 'You're *both* nuts,' she said matter-of-factly.

'Three people, Missy. Their names were Linh, Nathan, and Rose.'

Missy brushed crumbs off her lap and stood up. 'Rose didn't die here. She died in a car crash. I got told that on day one.'

'That's not what she says,' Erica said.

Missy stared at her, wide-eyed. 'You what?'

'We've talked to Rose. She's a ghost. She told us the truth about her death. We want to get you out of here before any more accidents happen.'

Missy put her empty glass on her empty plate and carried them over to the dishwasher. 'Have you told Mum and Dad about this?'

'Not yet, but—'

'—you won't. Because they won't believe you either. Great joke, Erica, but it's gone far enough. There's nothing weird going on here at all.'

'But—'

'Come on and I'll get someone to open the treatment room and *show* you, if you don't believe me. There's nothing in there that can hurt anyone.' She marched down the hallway towards her room. Erica and Toby followed, neither of them quite sure what to do next. They hadn't been sure that Missy would believe them without some persuasion or proof, but this flat denial was nonetheless strange.

Missy paused in her doorway. 'Weird,' she said.

'What?' Erica and Toby asked in unison.

'The door's already open. Usually they keep it shut during visiting hours.' She led the way in, flicking the light on as she did so.

The treatment room was small and bare. The floor and walls were padded, save for one, which had an opaque-looking window—probably one-way. There was a camera mounted up in one corner. A cupboard built into one wall popped open when Missy pushed the corner of its door. She reached in and brought out a pair of black goggles, and a pair of black gloves.

'That's virtual reality stuff,' Toby said, his voice sounding flat in the echoless room.

'Right. We wear these and they put us in the VR environment and we act out scenes designed to increase our tolerance to whatever it is we're afraid of. And that's the big secret, are you happy?' Missy flapped the gloves at them, and then put the goggles on; she looked like some kind of giant insect. 'There is nothing else going on at this place!'

'I'm afraid that's not quite true,' said Doctor Chapman, stepping into the room from behind Erica and Toby. She was accompanied by two men in the pale blue polo shirts that denoted staff members. 'We do have a rigorous program of treatment, and it produces some excellent results. I'm sure you'd like to contribute. Naturally, because we haven't pre-tested you, we don't know how suitable you'll be, but every experiment needs its outliers.'

The men stepped forward, one grabbing Erica by the arm, the other catching both of Toby's hands and pinning them behind his back. The gloves fell from Missy's fingers as she stared in shock.

'You can't do this!' Erica tried to yank her arm away. The man twisted it up almost to her shoulder blades and she yelped in pain as he pressed her against the wall.

'On the contrary, Ms. Sayle, I think that you'll find that we can.' Doctor Chapman looked at Missy. 'Put your gloves on please, Melissa. It's time for your next session.'

Erica kicked, but the man's grip was unbreakable. Doctor Chapman came forward and grasped Erica's free arm—Erica tried to hit her, but the doctor was too strong. She saw the needle before it went in and started screaming—and then everything dissolved into the darkness that Missy so feared.

CHAPTER SEVEN

When she opened her eyes again it was still dark, but there was a lambent green light emanating from somewhere off to her left that let her see two other people lying near her. It didn't take a genius to work out that they were Missy and Toby.

Erica rolled onto her stomach, levered herself up to her knees, and stopped there for a moment as her head spun sickly. She was kneeling on a hard surface that turned out to be rough stone when she brushed it with her fingertips.

'Missy? Toby?'

'Erica?' Missy responded immediately. She was sitting down, knees drawn up to her chest, but stood up and came over to Erica when Erica called her name. 'Are you all right?'

'I feel like someone hit me with a sledgehammer.'

'They drugged you both.'

'Where are we?'

'The mindscape,' Missy said. Erica must have looked puzzled, because she clarified: 'This is what the virtual reality has created for us. We've been linked in together.'

'Well, how do we get out?'

'We can't. The length of the session is determined by the doctors.' She sounded defeated.

'That's garbage. Hey!' Erica raised her voice. 'I know you're monitoring us! Let us out!'

Something chuckled thickly in the distance, and the light was blotted out for a moment as a large shape passed between it and them. Missy whimpered and Erica put an arm around her automatically. She was shaking like a leaf, and Erica didn't blame her—that laugh had not sounded even remotely human.

'Toby, wake up,' Erica said, kneeling beside him—her head span again—and shaking his shoulder.

Toby opened his eyes and blinked rapidly. 'What the hell? Where are we?'

'The mindscape,' Missy said again. 'It's a place they create out of our subconscious thoughts. Our fears. It's bad.'

'How do we get out?' Toby asked.

'We have to wait until they let us out.'

'Stuff that.'

'Yelling won't work. I've tried,' Erica said.

'They like it when I scream,' Missy said. She looked paler than ever in the eldritch green light. 'The worst part is it's *working*. People get better and go home. But if we tell ... if we tell anyone how bad it is, they'll disappear us like the others.'

'Well, stuff *them* then,' Toby said fiercely. 'Sit down here, both of you. We stay together, we don't react to anything, and they'll have to let us go if they don't get the reaction they want.'

Erica and Missy sat down beside him, the three of them huddling close together. They sat that way for maybe three minutes. The thing that laughed in the dark did it again, sounding closer this time.

'How big is this space?' Erica asked Missy.

'As big as it needs to be.'

That made sense. A wide space, such as this seemed to be, would do no good as a scary place for people like Rose, who were afraid only of being shut in. As a scary place for Missy, though, who was afraid of the things lurking on the edges of the darkness, it was perfect. She was still shaking, and Erica and Toby both put an arm around her, keeping her safe between them.

The green light unexpectedly went out. Erica strained her ears and eyes, but all was silent and still. Missy tensed up.

'Here it comes,' she whispered, throat almost closed with fear.

Suddenly the silence was shattered by the sound of a siren, screaming its warning through the darkness. Missy shrieked desolately and buried her face against Erica's shoulder, sobbing.

Erica tried closing her eyes tight and then opening them again, but all she could see was colours flashbulbing against the blackness from the pressure she had put on her eyes. 'Crap.'

'What?' Toby asked.

'Wish I could see.'

'Me too.'

'Me three,' Missy said.

The siren cut out as abruptly as it had begun. All three of them held their breath, waiting for the sound of something moving towards them through the dark. But the only sound was a perfectly innocuous one— water dripping from somewhere onto the stone that they were sitting on.

'Is that the best they can do?' Toby asked.

'I don't know what this is. This is new,' Missy said.

There was a light scraping noise from all around them. Erica reached out blindly, but touched only a stone wall.

'Wall's closer,' Toby said.

Erica got back up on her knees and shuffled around, keeping her hand on the wall. It had come closer all around, reducing their space to a circle of about eight feet in diameter. She put her hand up over her head and touched air; got to her feet and felt the ceiling just brushing her outstretched fingertips. The dripping water had turned into a trickle. She returned to her place and put her arm back around Missy. 'Are you claustrophobic too?'

'Not me,' Missy said.

'Not me,' Toby said.

'I know it's not me,' Erica said. 'Rose, are you in here with us?' There was no reply. 'Rose?' Toby let out a muffled exclamation. '*What?*'

'The water's touching me,' Toby said. 'It's cold. Soaking my jeans.'

'Stand up then.' She heard the soft splashing noise as he got to his feet, and heard Missy yelp as the water hit her as well, and scrambled to her own feet before it could wet her as well.

They all heard the trickle of water speed up, but Missy said anyway, 'It's getting faster.'

'It's coming in over here. There must be a hole,' Toby said. He splashed over to it. 'It's here.' The sound stopped. 'I've got my hand over it. The pressure's okay. It's not a very big hole.'

In the silence that followed, they all clearly heard the splashing when a second hole began letting more water in. Erica went to that one and covered it; she could feel it as a rough round hole in the rock, maybe two inches wide. Easy to cover with the palm of her hand. And when the third one opened beside her hip, spraying her with water, she covered that one as well.

'There's another one over here,' Missy's voice said to her left. 'Down near the floor.'

'I've got two here,' Erica said.

'Me too,' Toby said.

'Just one here—oh, wait—' Missy's hand slapped wetly over the hole in the darkness. 'Got it.' She paused. 'There's another one under my bum.' She squelched. 'Oh, yuck. I'm soaked.'

'I've got another one here too,' Toby said. 'I. Um. I'm running out of body parts to block this with.' He laughed, a high, thin sound.

Erica felt another one break open, squirting her neck, and leaned back, covering it with her shoulder. She could feel the water trickling down over her as if she were the weir up at Duncan's Creek. 'It's like the wall's rotting.'

'Mmmm. I hope it hurries up. The water's getting deeper,' Missy said, sounding far too calm. 'Not real. Not real.' It sounded like a mantra.

'Not real,' Erica echoed.

'There's one on the floor here,' Toby said.

'Use your foot.'

Toby splashed. It certainly *sounded* real. 'There. Got it.'

That was when the hole opened right over Erica's head. She yelped and pulled away, and was hit with a deluge as she uncovered all of the holes she had been blocking. She tried to rearrange herself so that she was covering all of them, but in order to reach the one over her head, she had to stretch, and then the one near her hip came uncovered. And there were more of them opening.

'I can't cover them all,' she said in a voice that surprised her with its calmness.

'Try and pull the wall down,' Toby said.

Although the holes were opening in the rock as if it were Swiss cheese, it was still totally solid.

'It's not real,' Missy said. 'Just remember that, it's not—' She screamed.

'Missy? Possum? What is it?' Erica left the wall and blundered towards the sound of Missy's voice.

'It's got me! It's got me!'

Erica groped along the wall, feeling for her sister. Found her. Ran her hand down Missy's arm. Her hand was in the hole. Her hand was in the wall, and something was in there with it, because Missy was shrieking, wordless panic resounding in the tiny chamber.

'Missy! Calm down! I'll get you out!' She tugged on Missy's hand, but Missy only screamed even louder, if that were possible.

'Stop! Erica, it's got me! Stop pulling, it'll take my hand!'

Toby splashed over to join them. The water was raining down hard from above. 'Missy, relax and let us try and get you out.'

'But it's *biting* me!'

'Curl your fingers and pull its jaw!'

Erica felt Missy's arm go tense, and then there was a horrible hurt squeal from the other side of the wall— God, she never wanted to see anything that sounded like that, it would have to be beyond hideous—and Missy's arm came free. She hugged it to her chest, whimpering, and Erica's gently exploring fingers felt the warm stickiness of blood. Missy still had the average number of fingers, though, which was a bonus.

With the holes unblocked, the water was pouring in merrily, and had risen to their knees. Erica kept pulling at one of the holes, trying to get the wall to fall down, but was wary of poking her fingers too far in after what had happened to Missy. Additionally, she wasn't sure if the wall falling in would just make more water flood the space that they were in, or whether whatever had bitten Missy would come through.

She couldn't see where the holes were in the dark, only feel them, and so when a pair of orange eyes opened about six inches from her face, and something hissed in the darkness beyond the hole, she jumped back and fell onto her backside.

'Damn!'

'What?' She felt Toby's hands, first blindly poking her back, and then sliding under her armpits to help her up. Now she was utterly soaked up to her waist, and more than a little wet above that from the water spraying out of the wall.

'Something's in there.' She heard Missy whimper. 'It's okay, possum.'

'How is it okay?' Missy said miserably. 'They're *watching* me. Waiting.'

'They're only watching, hon,' Toby said.

'That's what they do. And wait. And then when everyone else is gone, they—' Missy didn't finish the sentence, bursting into tears instead. Erica found her and put her arms around her.

'We're not going anywhere,' Toby said. 'We won't leave you alone with them.'

The water continued to pour in. Soon it was up to their waists, and the holes that were below the water's surface acted like large spa jets, buffeting them, almost knocking them over.

Impossibly, the eyes were still staring out of the hole Erica had seen them in. They had been joined by other sets of eyes blinking out of other holes. The sounds of gnashing teeth and hissing were audible even over the relentless sound of the water. Missy stopped crying and just huddled between Erica and Toby, not moving.

Before much longer, Erica realised she was having trouble breathing. The air seemed thin and bad. She opened her mouth wide, trying to inhale hard, and got splashed in the face.

'Gah!'

'What's wrong?' Toby asked.

'Is it just me or is the air going a little stale?'

'No, it's still good,' Toby said.

'Really? I can't—' Erica stopped and heaved another three quick breaths. 'It tastes like sea air. It didn't before.'

'The water's salty,' Missy said. 'It went in my mouth.'

'And the floor's just gone soft. Hold on.' Toby splashed in the darkness, duck-diving. He came back up spluttering a little. 'It's turned into sand.'

Erica felt the sand moving and shifting under her feet. The riptide was coming in. The rip. Dad had warned her about the rip, said not to go out too far, but Toby had said that they would be okay if they stayed close to shore, that they would still be able to get to the pier and back without going into the deeper water.

Her arms and legs were heavy. She was falling.

'Erica!'

She kicked off the bottom and rolled onto her back, spreading her arms out. 'Floating time,' she said. It was harder in clothes, but at least she was wearing light stuff. Toby, in jeans, wasn't faring as well. She could hear him splashing and cursing. Missy floated between them, light on the water.

Something solid and wet brushed against Erica's face and she shrieked in surprise.

'It's okay, it's just my jeans, I took 'em off.' Toby at least had the good grace to sound embarrassed.

They floated. The water was choppy, and Erica's head kept going under. She tried to balance herself with one hand against the wall, but the things moving behind the wall made her wary of staying in any one place for long. She reached up and touched the top of the cave. It was getting closer to her face. Couldn't be much longer before the water pushed them against the rock, and then came up over their bodies, and then they would ... well.

It's not real, it's not real, it's not real ...

The tip of her nose touched the rock, and she started screaming. She kicked and flailed and still the water rose inexorably. She could hear Toby telling her to calm down, and then Missy began screaming as well, as the things in the wall started coming out, little orange eyes on invisible bodies floating through the blackness, closer and closer. The hissing and the teeth-gnashing and the sound of the water pouring into the chamber, only ceasing when the water closed, at last, over Erica's head, filling her nose and mouth and lungs, filling her with liquid darkness.

CHAPTER EIGHT

When she opened her eyes again it was still dark, but a bit of sunlight filtered in through the canvas walls of the room—tent?—that they were in, enough to actually see by. Toby was lying on a sleeping bag to her left; Missy was curled into a ball at her feet. Erica herself was on a dull blue gym mat, completely dry.

Her clothes had changed; she now wore a black leotard and skin-tight Lycra leggings with a short purple spangly skirt over them. Missy wore a similar outfit, but her skirt was pink. Toby's clothes looked almost like a wetsuit, albeit a brightly coloured one. All three of them wore very soft shoes, almost like toughened socks, they were so thin and flexible.

Erica got to her feet and looked around. They were definitely in some sort of tent. The canvas was striped blue and white. Two big costume racks took up one side of the space, along with a large trunk overflowing with various bolts of sequinned fabric. There was a table with a sewing machine on it, surrounded by a tangle of cotton thread. Beside that was another trunk, this one full of juggling balls and batons and long cloth streamers and the like.

She woke the other two up as quickly as possible.

'No!' Toby nearly smacked her in the face. 'Oh. Sorry. Where *are* we?'

'I think it's a circus?'

'*Why?*'

'Clowns are a really common phobia.' Missy stood up. 'Something about the masks. The fake faces.'

'But *you* like them,' Erica said.

'Do *you*?' Missy looked at her, then at Toby. 'They don't have files on you. They're throwing whatever they have at you to see what gets a reaction.' She yanked the tent flap open.

At least Missy being mad was better than Missy being catatonic with fear.

They were in the middle of a field, surrounded by other tents and caravans. The view was dominated by one big tent, striped dark red and black, with a laughing clown's face painted on the panel closest to them. It looked a great deal like Missy's clown nightlight; Erica hoped Missy wouldn't notice. As Erica ventured further forward, she saw different things painted on the other panels: a man juggling, a woman hanging upside down on a trapeze, and an animal that looked like a badly rendered tiger.

Toby and Missy caught up with her. The three of them bunched together, holding hands with Missy in the middle, and edged between the tents. Everything was quiet, save for the sound of voices inside the big tent; it sounded like a restless crowd, but nothing that they were saying was specifically audible.

The trio were almost clear of the big tent when a tall man wearing a spangled suit and a top hat dashed through the main entrance and grabbed Toby's arm. 'Come on, you're meant to be performing now, not skulking around out here!' he snapped. Toby tried to pull away, but the man tightened his grip, and Toby gasped.

'Let him go!' Erica said.

'Don't you start with me, young lady. The audience have been waiting for five minutes already. If you don't get out there and perform, I'll drag you in there by the hair. Hell, I might do that anyway. Your act's getting dull. Nobody believes you're really putting yourself at risk, and so they think it's all rubbish.' He let go of Toby's arm and shoved him towards the tent entrance; Toby stumbled, swore, regained his footing, and turned to run.

'I don't think so, son,' a second man drawled from behind the first. This man held a leash. The leash was connected to a harness, and the harness was around what looked like approximately four hundred pounds of tiger. The tiger had probably been a white tiger once, but its fur was stained suspiciously red. It sat a pace behind its trainer like a tame dog and a growl rumbled deep in its chest. 'What say y'all get in there and do your thing now, huh?'

Toby limped forward and Erica and Missy had to follow, since the tiger looked like it hadn't eaten in about a week, judging by the way that it stared at them. The big tent smelled of sawdust, popcorn, tomato sauce, animal crap, and the avid sweaty smell of hundreds of people. They walked down a short space between two sets of wooden bleachers, seeing feet and ankles and then whole people. A couple of the spectators peered curiously over the railings at them. One of them spat into the sawdust at their feet and Missy made a sound of disgust; the man turned to face forward again, grinning an almost-toothless grin.

'Are you okay?' Erica asked Toby.

'Rolled my ankle.'

'Damn.'

'Shut up,' the first man said. 'Wait here. You'll hear your cue.' He went on ahead, leaving the tiger trainer to guard their only visible escape route. Well—not quite only. Erica judged that they could probably get under the bleachers and get a few metres start before the trainer could follow them, since it didn't look like the tiger would be able to scramble through the maze of support bars and struts under there.

She took two steps towards the bleachers anyway and heard the tiger's growl. It wasn't harnessed any more. It wasn't behind her any more, either. Sickly green eyes gleamed at her out of the darkness under the seats.

Erica opted to stop moving.

'This is so *wrong*,' Toby said, voice low and tight. 'Missy, how can they get away with this?'

'I don't think it's always been awful. I think they used to—'

She was interrupted by the rolling, booming voice of the ringmaster.

'Ladies and gentlemen, boys and girls, we here at the *Cirque de Peur* have a *very special* set of performers for you tonight! Please give them your *very best* welcome as they enter the ring! *Erica*, the Lady of the Air, trapeze artist extraordinaire!'

'I *what*?' Erica wasn't afraid of heights or falling, but she really wasn't a fan of hitting the ground.

'*Missy*, the Maiden of Motion, our acclaimed tightrope walker!'

'No. No way.' Missy took a step back and suddenly the tiger was behind them again, tail lashing across their calves.

'And *Toby*, Defyer of Gravity, who will not only demonstrate his prowess on the tightrope but do it while juggling!'

'This is—' Toby jumped as the tiger's teeth nearly closed on his thigh.

They looked back towards the tent's entrance one more time, but the tiger trainer motioned for them to go on, looking impatient. They walked out between the bleachers and into the blinding glare of the spotlights. The crowd's murmur rose to a roar of applause; Erica heard snarls and growls mixed in with the cheers.

There were two trapeze platforms set up. A man wearing similar clothing to Toby's stood atop one, holding his trapeze in one hand. Erica had no idea what she was expected to do, but there was a shimmering safety net stretched below the trapeze area and another one below the tightrope. Whatever was meant to evoke fear here, maybe it wasn't the idea of falling onto dirty sawdust and snapping her neck.

'I can't,' she said. 'I won't.'

The tiger growled.

'Suit yourself,' the tiger trainer said. 'But he hasn't eaten in a week.' His grin showed teeth as menacing as the tiger's. 'Neither have I.'

'Not real,' Missy whispered, voice failing.

Real or not, the trapeze suddenly looked less scary than the tiger.

Erica climbed the thin ladder to the top of the platform. It was a long way to the ground, and for a moment she considered just sitting down and refusing to do anything more, but as she hesitated she saw the tiger trainer look up at her—then at the tiger and Missy.

The threat was clear.

She unhooked the trapeze bar from the edge of the platform, watching the man on the opposite platform carefully. He smiled cheerily and gave her a thumbs-up, and she tried to smile back before gripping the trapeze. He stepped off the platform and she mimicked him with one last glance to where the tiger was breathing on the backs of Missy's legs.

Mid-air, he released the bar and turned a tight somersault before hooking the bar back to him, this time with his knees. He grabbed her hands and suddenly her bar was gone and she was flying with only his hands holding her up. They swung back towards his platform, past it, and back into the centre of the tent.

That was when he let her go.

Erica shrieked and the crowd clapped. She tucked her knees to her chest as she went flying backwards, and then suddenly her trapeze was there and she caught it, sweaty fingers only barely managing to hold the grip, and the crowd moaned as if deprived of a favourite toy. She swung out and then back again. This time the man caught her by the ankles. She clung to her trapeze. The man snarled and tugged her body towards him, one hand holding her ankles firmly together, the other reaching for her nerveless fingers.

He pulled one finger back until her muscles stretched agonisingly, and the bone let go with a snap. Erica screamed as pain flooded her whole arm. She let go of the bar, and he dropped her again and the whole crazy scene flew past her as she plummeted headfirst towards the net, trying to cradle her head with her hands, certain that the net would break and she would fall the rest of the way to the sawdust ring.

She hit the net, bounced back a little way, and then lay still, flat on her back, sobbing in fear and shock and anger.

The crowd had fallen silent save for a few anticipatory murmurs. Her partner had swung back to his platform; he took a single bow and then crouched, pulling up on a cord that she had not previously noticed. A large box attached to the tower he was standing on opened, and the crowd let out a long, '*Ahhhh,*' as if he'd pulled a rabbit out of a hat.

Except it wasn't a hat, and it sure as hell wasn't a rabbit.

A giant spider advanced towards her.

Erica rolled to get up and bail over the side—if she dropped just right, she might get away with only a pair of broken ankles.

That was when she realised the reason that the net was shimmering was because it wasn't a net, it was a huge spider web, and she was stuck to it. She pulled frantically at the sticky strands as the spider moved down the web, taking its time; it knew she wasn't going anywhere.

'Erica! *Erica! Noooo!*'

She got one hand free and then its fangs sank into her shoulder, numbing the area instantly. *Well, maybe my broken finger will stop hurting,* she thought inanely, trying to kick her legs free, but failing as the poison gradually anaesthetised her whole body. The spider pulled her free of the web and began to wrap her up in less sticky but tougher strands of silk. To her bleary eyes it looked like a funnelweb, but due to how oversized it was it could just as easily have started off as a tiny money spider.

It didn't matter what sort of spider it was, though; it had her, she was gone, she was dead.

The spider rolled her to the edge of the web and hung her head-down, and then retreated to the centre of the web. Erica felt the blood rush to her head but she was already dizzy and drowsy from the bite and it made no difference anyway ... no difference ...

She could vaguely see Toby and Missy and the tiger trainer; the trainer was prodding Missy forward and Missy went, climbing the ladder to the tightrope, balancing out over the void. She took tiny steps and made it right across, to the displeasure of the crowd. She saluted the crowd at the other end, both hands going up the same way that they had when she'd done gymnastics when she was little, before puberty had hit and her newly gawky body had been too clumsy to continue competing.

Then she flipped the crowd the bird, middle fingers rising from her fists.

Toby went up, the tiger no longer growling but snapping at his heels. Erica's trapeze partner followed him, solemnly handing him a set of juggling balls before nudging him forward onto the rope.

They know what scares you. They get it from your brain.

The words were whispered *inside* her head, not heard with her ears, and she tried vainly to identify the voice as the roar of the crowd grew. The male trapeze artist was pushing Toby harder as he refused to step out onto the rope. Missy raised her hands, palms up, beckoning him forward.

Erica's vision was going blurry from the poison and her inverted position, but she saw what happened next in crystal clear slow motion.

Toby stepped out onto the rope, holding the juggling balls—two in one hand, one in the other. They were all coloured dark red. He walked a few paces forward and then stopped. It was a proper tightrope, not a steep slack rope, but it didn't look very thick. He moved forward again. The male trapeze artist bent down and gave the rope a little wiggle, and Toby cast a scared look over his shoulder and then moved forward another few steps.

'You can do it, Toby!' Missy called, seeming to be impossibly distant.

'Can he?'

The ringmaster was standing near Erica where she dangled at the edge of the web.

'Can he?' he repeated. 'Does he have what it takes?'

Erica felt like her mouth was full of cotton wool; she couldn't respond.

The ringmaster cracked his whip terrifyingly close to her face, and Toby looked down, tottered, and then lifted his hands. He squeezed the juggling balls together and red liquid poured out of them down his arms. He cast them away in disgust and the gesture knocked him off balance.

Erica tried to scream but only got a mouthful of spider silk as Toby fell, arms and legs pinwheeling. He hit the net and kept going as first it stretched and then snapped, made of nothing stronger than ordinary sewing cotton.

The sound when he hit the ground was like dropping a pumpkin onto concrete.

She saw his head snap up and down again and heard his neck break, heard the crowd screaming with rapture and Missy screaming in terror as she scrambled down the long ladder and ran to him. Toby lay very still on the sawdust, his eyes open and fixed on her, his limbs spreadeagled but not even twitching after that impact.

That was when the clowns came in.

Their car was painted black and red like everything else. Their costumes were the stuff of nightmares—Erica saw a belt of bones, a tight bodysuit made to look like flayed muscles, a wig made of real human scalps. They piled out of the car, running to surround Toby and Missy, honking horns that let out the sounds of screaming and crying, throwing custard pies that bled, squirting blood out of the macabre dead flowers pinned to their lapels.

And all of them wore masks. Grinning masks, surprised masks, sad masks, but all twisted, mocking the emotions that they represented.

One of them held aloft a giant saucepan and wooden spoon, banging them together. 'Food's up!' it hollered. 'Time to dine!'

The crowd were silent, on the edge of their seats.

Black roses were blooming in front of Erica's eyes.

The circle closed.

As the darkness descended, she heard them begin to feed.

CHAPTER NINE

When she opened her eyes again it was still dark, but she found Toby easily enough in spite of not being able to see. He was beside her, curled into a foetal position, whimpering, 'Their teeth! They hurt! Stop biting stop biting stop stop stop ...' Erica touched him and he screamed. 'No! Stop!' His voice died to a horrified whisper. 'Where are your faces?' On his other side Missy moved in the darkness, a sleepy murmur turning into a terrified gasp. Erica found Toby's hand and squeezed it tightly; reached across him and caught Missy's hand and held it.

'It's me, you guys, it's okay, you're alive.'

'It's so *not* okay,' Missy sniffled, but she squeezed Erica's hand. Toby's free arm went awkwardly around Erica's waist from underneath. They stayed that way for a moment, and then disentangled themselves.

'Where are we now?' Toby asked, voice still raw and shaky.

'The right way up, thank God,' Erica said.

'No God,' Missy said. 'Not in here.'

'When we get out of here we're going straight to church,' Erica said.

'If we get out of here,' Toby said. 'They managed to disappear three other people before us.'

'Well, then, shut up before you give them ideas,' Erica said. She bounced a little. 'I think we're sitting on a bed.'

'We are,' Missy said. 'I'm sure that doesn't surprise you.'

It didn't. Not really. First Erica had drowned, and then Toby had been killed by masked monsters. Now this was Missy's scene, Missy's nightmare. Never mind that she had already been going through this for a week. It was out of their hands and in the hands of whoever controlled the scenario, whether it was Doctor Chapman, Doctor Morley, or one of the nameless, blue-shirted orderlies.

'What happens?' Erica asked.

Missy scootched up the bed. 'I don't know. It changes each time. Maybe with you guys here it won't be so bad.' She didn't sound particularly hopeful about the prospect.

Erica also shifted up the bed until she bumped into the headboard. It was solid wood—no, not quite solid, because when she ran her hand over it there were two gaps. Three thick, wide, horizontal bars, then—the sort of solid headboard that belonged to either a homemade bedframe or a bedframe made from some rare wood, bought from an expensive shop, polished to within an inch of its life.

She would give anything for this bed to turn into her bed, right now, and for this to all just be a dream, ideally beginning about six months ago. Then she could go and blow the damned Fear Clinic up before it even opened, although that would doubtless make people wonder why she had done so.

'Erica, are you still there?' Missy asked.

'Right here, possum.'

'You went quiet.' Missy scrambled over Toby to settle between the two of them.

'Just thinking.'

'Oh.'

'It's an unusual occurrence,' Toby confided to Missy in a stage whisper, 'and so that's probably why you didn't recognise it.' Erica hit him and for a second things seemed almost normal.

Then the whispering started.

In the shadows, just beyond the edge of the bed, low voices conferred with each other over an unknown matter of great importance. Their voices were sibilant, the words impossible to make out—not English, not any language Erica had ever heard, and considering that they had gone on several overseas holidays, she had heard a few. The tone seemed urgent, but maybe that was just because the words sounded as if they were being run together, unnecessary words, even phrases, being dropped. There were no faces to go with the voices, not even glowing eyes as there had been in the cave.

A threatening low growl sounded over the babble of voices, which abruptly stopped. The growl was familiar, something Erica had heard before, but chilling nonetheless. She racked her brain trying to think of what it could be. It evoked a faint memory of sitting in the car outside a restaurant with Missy, waiting for her parents to finish their conversation and come drive them home.

'That's a possum,' Toby said.

As soon as he said it, Erica remembered. It had been the first time that they had heard the growl of a possum during mating season, and it had scared Missy into inconsolable sobs. Now, though, she just laughed, albeit a little nervously.

'They're going to have to do better than that this time.'

A hand slid onto Erica's right shoulder and she reached up to pat it comfortingly, assuming that it was Missy's. Her fingers encountered solid wooden fingers that flexed open and snapped shut around her hand. She uttered a little cry of surprise and reached up with her right hand to try and pry her left hand free, but the wooden hand's grip was unshakable. Tracing it back as far as she could reach, she thought it might be growing out of the headboard.

'Um, guys,' she said, trying to sound calm, 'I'm a bit stuck here.'

'What? Why?' Missy asked.

'There's a wooden hand and it's grabbed my hand.'

'Can you pull free?' Toby asked.

'No. It's too tight.' And tightened more every time she tried to get loose.

'Ow!' Toby yelped.

'What?'

'It's got my *hair*!' His weight on the bed shifted. 'Ow, no, pulling free bad idea, bad idea, ow.' His voice shook. 'There's another one. Got my wrist. Missy, *move*, they're everywhere up here.'

Erica dropped her right hand back down by her side as Missy started scrambling, and another wooden hand shot out of the headboard and pinioned it. She tried to pull that hand loose and stopped when the wooden hand squeezed so tightly that it felt as if her wristbones were grinding together.

'I'm really stuck,' she said.

'Me too,' Toby said.

'I'm not.' Missy moved down, stopping somewhere near Erica's knees. 'Now they won't get me.' Her voice changed. 'No. No! My foot!' She kicked at something in the darkness; Erica felt the thudding vibrations. Then the bedsheets were sliding out from under her as something dragged Missy away and Missy clung to whatever she could grab to stop herself going. Her fingertips brushed Erica's ankle and then were gone.

'Missy? Missy!'

'*Mine*,' said a voice from the darkness. Maybe it *was* the darkness. It sounded like it was stifling laughter.

'No!' Erica pulled against the grasping hands and only succeeded in nearly dislocating her right shoulder. 'Give her back!'

'*Mine*,' the voice said again. Missy screamed in the darkness. There was the sound of footsteps going out of the room and a door closing. Missy screamed again, further away. Then she was gone.

'How the hell do we get out of this?' Toby asked.

'Have you got a free hand? See if you can find something. A light, or something to break these fingers with.' She heard his fingers pattering across something—wood, but not the headboard, he wouldn't touch the headboard and risk getting grabbed—and then the click of a switch. Low light flooded the room from a familiar clown-shaped nightlight; Erica screwed her eyes shut and tried to lift her hands to cover them.

'Sorry,' Toby said. 'I didn't think.'

'It's okay,' Erica said, wondering what she was going to see when she opened her eyes.

It turned out to be a perfectly ordinary bedroom. Bed, nightstand, chest of drawers, wardrobe, desk, chair, clotheshorse, four walls, ceiling, floor, door, the whole bit. There was a dressing gown hanging on the back of the door that probably looked a bit like a person in the right sort of dim light. The wardrobe door hung open just enough of a crack to showcase the darkness and shadowy shapes inside that would, with the door all the way open, prove to be nothing more than a jumble of shoes and coats.

The kneehole of the desk had an abandoned teddy bear in it with glass eyes that sparkled in the lamplight just enough that, if seen out of the corner of the eye, they would look like something living, and of course the clotheshorse, placed over a central heating duct, bore clothes that fluttered just a bit in the rush of warm air so that if someone caught sight of them when their eyes had adjusted to the darkness after the lights went out they might seem like a lurking creature readying itself to pounce. But they were only normal, mundane things, and if not for the wooden hands still holding her and Toby firmly against the headboard, she would have thought that this was an ordinary teenager's bedroom.

Toby had continued prospecting over the nightstand and had found something he thought would help, judging by his satisfied, 'Ah!' of discovery. She heard the woody shuffle of matches in a box.

'Let's see if this gets 'em to let go,' he said. He pulled out a match and put the box between his teeth to hold it so that he could strike the match. It flared brightly, a force against the shadows, and Toby lowered it to hold it against the hand holding his right wrist. The hand uncurled and pulled back as soon as the heat touched it, and Toby grinned triumphantly, and then transferred the match to his newly freed hand and reached up behind his own head to free his scalp.

As soon as he was free he scrambled down the bed out of reach of any further attacks (at least theoretically—the baseboard was pretty big as well), shook the match out, and lit a fresh one to apply to Erica's captors. He leaned very close to do so, and Erica couldn't help but think that if they were in a movie, this would be the moment that they would discover their previously unmentioned but deep-rooted attraction to one another and engage in a passionate kiss.

It was probably lucky that they weren't in a movie, because such a scene would have been ruined by the helpless giggling that overcame her.

'I can't believe you're laughing,' Toby said. 'What's the joke?'

'Nothing, nothing,' Erica said, rubbing her wrist as Toby freed it. Then she thought of a plausible excuse. 'I was just thinking that if they could make this bed in the real world, they could shut down the Fear Clinic and open up an adult store.'

'Yuck,' Toby said, applying the match to the hand holding her left hand. 'There.'

'Thanks. I was getting a cramp.' 'Do you need a massage?'

'I think we need to go find Missy,' Erica said. She got up off the bed, and then was struck by a thought. 'Were there candles with those matches?'

Toby rolled off his side of the bed and, after a brief search, found candles in the nightstand drawer. The candles were fat round pillars with some sort of herbs stuck to them. She turned on the overhead light and found a piece of cardboard in one of the desk drawers to make drip catchers, which she fitted around two of the candles. There was one each, and Toby put two spare ones in his pocket—his jeans had reappeared at some point, and so they were back to the clothes they had begun with. The only other candles were tealights, and they were difficult to carry easily without some sort of proper holder to keep from getting burnt.

As well as the candles, she found a tennis racquet amongst the jumble of things in the wardrobe, and Toby picked up a heavy glass paperweight from the computer desk.

When it came time to open the door out into the hallway—or whatever it was that lay beyond the door, although given that Missy had been carried out there, Erica assumed that there was at least *some* sort of passageway to another place—she found herself to be strangely reluctant. She put her hand on the knob, but simply wondering what the darkness beyond the door would hold kept her from turning it.

'Go on, Erica,' Toby said. 'I've got your back.'

'It's my front I'm worried about.' She moved to one side of the door, turned the knob to ease the lock-tongue free, and then tossed the door open, grabbing the tennis racquet's handle in the same downward movement.

There was nothing out there except ... *hallway*. It had a black and white chequered linoleum floor and the walls were draped with red cloth, with the occasional carefully shielded sconce containing a larger version of the candles they were carrying, but there was nothing in it. It stretched out of sight to both the left and the right. There were no doorways, no stairs, no breaks in the bland red expanse save for the sconces.

Toby blew out his candle right away, but Erica kept hers alight. She carried it carefully in her right hand, the racquet in her left; though she was right-handed, she figured she could swing the racquet okay with her wrong hand, preferring to have the candle under control so that it wouldn't go out.

'Left or right?' she asked.

'I wouldn't go either way,' Toby said.

'Just *pick* one.'

'Left, then. That was a movie quote, by the way. *Labyrinth*. Although I wouldn't expect you to have seen it, since the scariest thing in it was David Bowie's crotch.'

Erica poked him with the tennis racquet. 'You can lead the way, smart guy.'

Toby set off down the hallway, striding along apparently unafraid. Only the way he walked a little more cautiously than usual—and this was from a boy who had been known to hurtle merrily off down ski slopes two levels higher than his skill called for—gave away the fact that he was at least a bit nervous.

Erica was more than a bit nervous. Toby was the one facing up to the unknown, but she caught herself glancing over her shoulder every two seconds to see what might be slinking up behind them. The light from the open bedroom door dwindled into the distance as they walked, and eventually became just another point of light amongst the candles, and still they hadn't found any sort of door or stairwell or opening.

'It just goes on and on,' Toby murmured. Then he stopped abruptly in the middle of the hallway, turned to face one of the walls, and ran his hand along it.

'Aha!' He stepped forward, nose against the red fabric, and then stepped sideways, vanishing into the wall. 'I guess you *can't* take anything for granted in this place,' he said, poking his head and hand back out of the wall. 'Come on.'

Erica ran the tennis racquet along the wall and found the place where it stopped immediately. Once she was on exactly the right angle it became visible. They'd been looking for obvious doorways, but this was well concealed.

'Nice one, Toby.'

'Thank you.'

The new hallway was panelled with dark wood; the light here came from brass candleholders, set further apart than the sconces had been in the other hallway. It was a shorter hallway, too—Erica could see a doorway up ahead outlined by a very faint light. Two paintings hung on the wall, one on either side of the doorway. One was of a woman wearing white, lying down with a demon sitting on her chest grinning, and a pale horse with glowing eyes—Erica recognised it as Fuseli's *Nightmare*. Her enthusiastic analysis of the elements of the picture hadn't gone down at all well in art class—but she had barely turned to face the other painting when a pair of hands pressed against it from the inside, as if someone trapped in the painting was trying to get out.

'Scary stuff from a computer game released fifteen years ago doesn't cut it,' she said, and the hands went back into the wall as if abashed by her words. 'Neither does anything I've ever written an in-depth essay on,' she added to the other picture, and the demon dropped the little knife it was holding and burst into tears, which was a little unexpected.

She turned her attention to the door. It was breathing. That was okay—a typical scare tactic. The doorknob was warm, but not too hot, and that was also okay. Toby jostled her a little and murmured an apology.

'Just be ready,' Erica said, and she turned the knob and shoved the door open.

The room beyond was a waiting room. The walls and carpet and hard plastic chairs were all beige. The reception desk was not staffed and a door beside it was discreetly marked *Surgery*. As rooms went, it was bland and not at all the sort of thing that Erica had been expecting. With Toby behind her, she crossed the room and opened the next door.

Where *nothing* was okay.

Missy was lying on what looked like a stainless steel hospital gurney in the middle of the room, wearing a plain white hospital robe. She had black gloves on and dark goggles—Erica recognised them as the equipment that Missy had shown them in the treatment room. A computer monitor showed Missy's brainwaves, the slow steady delta waves of deep sleep. Her heart rate, in a corner of the same monitor, was normal.

This was interesting, because as far as Erica could see, Missy was not hooked up to anything that was measuring any such rhythms.

She stepped up to the bed and lifted the goggles carefully off Missy's face. Missy was staring blankly straight upwards, but didn't react when Erica removed the goggles. Erica pulled the gloves off and tried to get Missy to wake up. There was no reaction. Eyes open or not, she was definitely deep asleep.

'Here, let me,' Toby said. He shoved the paperweight into his pocket as far as it would go, and lifted Missy into his arms. 'Where do we go?'

'Nowhere,' said a voice from the other side of the room. A man in a white lab coat, his face hidden by a surgical mask, had entered through an archway that led into a second, darkened room. 'You can't take her away now. We need to open her up and see what makes her the way she is.'

'No way,' Erica said, hefting the tennis racquet.

The man moved forward, lifting an item of his own—a shiny scalpel. 'Then it will be all three of you, and we will find out what makes you tick.' He walked past a desk piled high with papers and manila folders, and a tall filing cabinet. 'Put her back on the table.'

Erica glanced down involuntarily and saw that the gurney was actually an autopsy table, with a trough around the edge for drainage, and even a little sink built into it. White porcelain; rusty plug hole.

Maybe rust, anyway.

'No.' This time her protest was a lower moan as she struggled not to think of what the man's intentions were. 'You can't have her.'

She looked back up and saw that the man in the white coat was closer.

'But she's mine,' he said. 'Some people just don't read their paperwork properly.'

'No. She's mine. My family. My blood.'

'Really?' the man said contemplatively. 'May I see the blood in question?'

Toby did put Missy back down, but only so that he could pull the paperweight from his pocket and throw it smoothly at the man, aiming for his forehead. The man reached up and batted it away. 'Don't be foolish,' he said. 'Resistance will gain you nothing.'

'Get stuffed,' Toby said.

The man ignored him. 'I may make you watch,' he added thoughtfully.

'Monster,' Erica hissed, as Toby picked Missy back up. She moved towards the doctor, lifting the racquet as if to serve a ball straight at his head. The threat didn't stop him in the least.

The pile of papers suddenly flying off the desk and hitting him in the back did, though. He fell to his knees, and Erica clubbed him over the head with the edge of the racquet, wondering why the papers had flown, but not questioning it too much. She took a step back to swing again and was pushed further back by invisible hands before the tall filing cabinet began to creak and sway. It toppled forward, vomiting its drawers out onto the man before landing atop him. He screamed in surprise and pain and then was silent.

Rose was standing where the filing cabinet had been, a little less transparent now. 'I can help you in here,' she said, 'and I can help you out there a little, but once you get out, you're on your own.' She held up one hand. 'I'm fading.' Her voice was young and soft and sad.

'Hang in there,' Erica said. 'We'll help you—we'll expose the truth.'

'You need to find a way into the basement,' Rose said. 'I didn't see which way they took me in, because I was dead then, but you'll find it. I have faith in you.' She smiled. 'You're all so strong.'

Erica reached out to her, but touched only air as her fingers passed through Rose's. 'Oh, hon, I'm so sorry,' she said, her voice choking up.

'Be sorry later. They're about to let you go. They can't see what's going on any more because we interfered with their computers. You need to be ready.'

'We?'

Two other ghosts appeared on the other side of the autopsy table. The woman—Linh, Erica guessed— looked to be in her early thirties, with long dark hair and a disbelieving look as she stared down at the unmoving body under the filing cabinet. Nathan, the boy that Rose had spoken about, appeared to be only thirteen or fourteen. Blond-haired and blue-eyed, he looked more bewildered than anything else.

'We've found that we can have a small effect on electrical equipment,' Rose said. 'We're not strong though, and the more that we do, the less we can *keep* doing. Understand?'

Toby nodded. So did Erica. Missy remained unmoving in Toby's arms.

'Get ready. It's time.'

Everything faded to black.

CHAPTER TEN

They were all lying on the padded floor of the treatment room, and Erica clawed the goggles and gloves off with feverish haste, driven by the desire to rid herself of every last vestige of those horrible scenarios. *This* was the real world. She knew that as well as she knew that her middle name was Jane, and that if she didn't trim her hair soon her split ends would take over the planet.

Beside her, Toby had also torn off his goggles and gloves and was helping Missy off with hers. Doctor Chapman was absent from the room, but Erica felt certain the woman wasn't far away—perhaps behind the one-way glass, or watching them through the camera. Likewise, the orderlies had gone, though Erica could hear someone on the other side of the closed door.

'We need to go now and go fast,' she said.

'What about Rose's proof?' Toby asked.

'I think we need to worry about that some other time,' Erica said. 'Like when nobody knows we're here.' The first glimmerings of a plan were already forming themselves in her head, but after the panic and terror they'd just been through, she didn't want to spend a second longer than necessary in this Godforsaken place.

Toby opened the door and went through, ploughing past the two orderlies who moved to block his path, sending them staggering against the wall. Erica helped Missy, who was stumbling. They burst out into the hallway and sprinted towards the front doors, hearing a commotion from inside Missy's room as the orderlies regrouped and followed them. But, as slowed as they were from their experiences, the trio made it to the front door first, flashing past Jocelyn, who stared at them open-mouthed, galloping down the front steps, and hurling themselves into Toby's car. Toby started the car and had them out on the road in seconds, taking the corners at sixty miles an hour and not slowing down until they hit the long flat stretch between Centralia and Lilywood. It was only two-thirty according to the dashboard clock; it felt as if they had been in there forever.

In the back seat, Missy hugged Erica with feverish intensity. 'Thank you, thank you, thank you,' she almost chanted.

'Why didn't you tell us you wanted to come home if that was happening?' Erica couldn't help asking.

'They wouldn't let me. They said that if I asked to come home they'd come and get me in the middle of the night and then the monsters would be real,' Missy said. She burst into tears. Erica leaned forward, hooked tissues out of the gap between the driver's seat and front passenger seat, and handed them to her sister.

'None of it is real, everything they did to you is wrong, and we're going to go back there and prove that they're responsible for Rose's death. Linh and Nathan too. There's got to be proof. If that autopsy room is real, like Rose said, we'll find it and we'll get their files. She was showing us what to look for.'

'How are you planning to get back in?' Toby asked. 'Do you know where to go once you get in there? And what are you going to do with the proof once you find it? That's what I want to know.'

'I think the entrance must be through the hallway where Chapman's office is. The door in the simulation corresponded to that door behind reception. I thought that if one of us snuck in and set off a fire alarm, then we could get in through a side door or window while everyone was evacuating. We get in, grab the files, and get out. Go straight to the police in Centralia, hand the files over, and let them take it from there.'

'I hope it's that straightforward,' Toby said, making the left turn onto the Lilywood road. 'I don't fancy the idea of the police arresting us for breaking and entering.'

'That's why we find an *open* door to go in through,' Erica said.

'There's a little bit more to it than that.'

'I know, I know. But they'll be so pleased that we've got the proof ...'

'Wouldn't it be better to go to them without the proof and have them go in?' Missy piped up. 'I don't want to go back in there.'

'They're not going to believe us!' Toby said. 'It's too wild a story. We can't just rock up and say "oh yeah, we were drugged and put through psychological torture, we don't really know why other than that they're doing some sort of experiment so unethical it would make Philip Zimbardo think it was a bit much, can you go arrest them please?". If the police did bother to go question the staff, it turns into them against us, and we're going to wind up institutionalised for real.'

They debated the pros and cons of each option all the way back to the Sayle house, but the debate was cut short as the car turned into the driveway. Erica saw her parents waiting for them outside the front door, arms folded, not smiling.

'Uh oh,' she said.

Uh oh turned out to be an understatement.

'The clinic called us,' their father said, as soon as Erica and Missy got out of the car. 'Just what did you think you were doing?'

'What did *we* think we were doing? What did *they* think they were doing?' Erica demanded. 'They drugged Toby and I and put us into their twisted virtual reality!'

'That's not what Doctor Chapman said,' their mother said. 'She said that you and Toby burst in and dragged Missy out when she was in the middle of her lunch.'

'We would have, if they hadn't *attacked* us,' Erica said.

'I find it very hard to believe,' said their father.

'Look.' Erica pointed to the fading pinprick on her upper arm where the needle had gone in. 'Can't you see?'

'I can't see anything except a young woman who has got some serious explaining to do. Tobias, you'd better come inside as well. I've called your parents—' Toby let out a groan '—and they'll be coming over shortly. The three of you can tell your story when everyone's here.'

'But Dad,' Erica began.

'No buts. Inside.'

They filed silently into the formal living room. Not much living got done there—the occasional afternoon tea with a client, sipping tea and nibbling biscuits, careful not to drop crumbs, not that the girls were allowed into the room if either of their parents was having a meeting in there.

Erica sat on one of the couches. Missy sat beside her. Toby sat on the other end of the couch and fidgeted until the doorbell rang and his parents came in, and then he folded his hands in his lap and just jiggled one leg a little bit.

Once their parents were all settled, the inquisition started, and Erica realised just how hard it was to explain why she had even gone up there without sounding insane. She mentioned Rose, but only as far as the car accident went, and said nothing the ways that Rose had spoken to her. She mostly just stuck to her story of how she had felt that Missy looked as if she was getting worse rather than better, and the other two kept their mouths shut except for the occasional word of agreement.

To give them credit, their parents didn't say anything until she had finished her stumbling explanation, but the silence was in a way worse than if they had been blustering in disbelief. Her father shook his head all through the part about them being drugged. She skimmed over their shared mindscape, mostly because she felt like it was a private thing, especially given how embarrassed Toby looked when she got to the part about the circus. At last she finished with them running out of the clinic and driving home, and then she sat back, pulled a stiff embroidered cushion onto her lap, and wrapped her arms around it.

'It's certainly a wild story,' her father said. 'I can understand you being worried about your sister. But for God's sake, Erica, there had to be a better way to express your feelings than this.'

'I didn't really think. I just went,' Erica said, eyes downcast.

'Well, that's obvious. The least you could have done was waited until we came home and discussed your feelings with us. As for this nonsense about the girl who was in the car accident, I simply don't know where to begin. What gave you the idea to look her up in the first place?'

'I was googling the Fear Clinic to see what other people might have said about it and ran across the obituary that way,' Erica said. She wished that she *had* googled the place months ago, instead of relying on the word of mouth that her parents had accepted so readily. 'Then it seemed strange that a car accident could happen on that stretch of road and the bodies be so badly burned before anyone got there to help. It's not exactly the middle of nowhere, even on a Sunday afternoon.'

'And reading this article made you think that Missy was in danger for some reason.'

'Not exactly. You know what? Forget about the obituary.' Rose wouldn't like that, if she was around, but Erica couldn't help that. 'It's not relevant. I went up to get Missy because she looked like she'd slept half as much as usual. She looked like she'd been through hell and back. And after what we went through in their damned virtual reality scenarios, I can understand why she looked like that.'

She looked down at her hands, clutching the cushion, and then up again at her parents. 'I didn't think I was afraid of anything and their program showed me that I was. For someone like Missy, who *knows* what they're afraid of, it must be a thousand times worse.'

'And what was your part in all this, Tobias?' Mr. Noonan asked.

'I drove Erica up there and went in with her. I hadn't seen Missy before, but as soon as I saw her there, I knew what Erica meant. Missy was so well and happy when she came to the bonfire night at our house. When I saw her sitting there at the clinic, she looked like she'd died and been brought back.'

'So you helped bring her out.'

'After they shot me full of God knows what and I went through the scene, the nightmare, whatever you want to call it.'

Mrs. Noonan looked at Erica's mother. 'He's never told anyone but us about his fear of masks. He hasn't even told his brother. How could the people at the clinic find that out?'

'They look in your head,' Missy said. 'Sort of. They look at your brainwaves, and they try lots of different things to see what makes you have that fear reaction. They tried heights and spiders on us as well before they sent in the clowns. They have a checklist. I've seen it. If that hadn't worked, the next scene would have had us attacked by snakes, or getting terminally ill, or trapped in a fire.'

'Well,' said Erica's father. 'It's certainly a very convoluted tale. Why don't you kids go in the back room and play Scrabble while we talk?'

Erica could tell he didn't believe them, but got up dutifully and walked out of the room, Toby and Missy trailing her. She could hear their parents starting to talk in low voices before she'd even gotten to the kitchen. It was okay. They'd come up with their own explanation, one that probably involved very little of what she had told them, and then she could get on with getting her evidence at a later stage. She wished that she hadn't mentioned Rose. Now they would be wondering why she had. Still, it was too late now.

They settled themselves around the coffee table—Erica and Toby on either end of the battered old couch, Missy sprawled out on the red corduroy beanbag that she'd made herself in some Fibres and Fabrics class or other. WEAK. COME NOW was still written on the Scrabble board.

'Rose did that?' Missy asked.

'Yeah,' Erica said.

'Fair enough. Is she here now?'

'I don't think so,' Erica said. 'She'd be writing something if she were.'

For lack of anything else to do, they put all of the tiles back in the bag and then started a new game. Toby was ahead by twenty-three points when the sound of footsteps stopped them.

'Come on, Toby, we're going home,' Mrs. Noonan said.

Toby didn't say anything, but got up right away, patting Erica's shoulder on his way past.

'See you, Toby,' Erica said.

'Bye, Toby,' Missy said.

'Bye.' He didn't sound nearly as happy as he usually did. He was probably anticipating some serious questioning in the car on the way home.

The Noonans left. It wasn't until their car had pulled out of the driveway and the sound of its engine had faded away down the road that Erica dared to ask, 'What did you decide?'

'That if Missy wants to be home so badly, she might as well stay. We'll pick her things up another time, since their visiting hours are over up there.' Their mother gave her a look that, to Erica's surprise, was pitying. 'Next time, don't make up stories. Just tell us what's wrong. Then you won't need to carry on like this. I know we've been paying a lot more attention to Missy than to you, but you're twenty-two. You should be old enough to not need our attention all the time.'

Erica opened and shut her mouth, thinking, *if this were a book or a movie, I'd be protesting my innocence right about now*. Instead, she didn't say anything in her own defence, only offering up, 'Well, in that case, I'd better cook dinner. What does everyone want?'

'I think a barbecue would be a good idea now that the rain's passed,' her father said. 'We've got those fresh chicken satays we found while we were shopping. I'm dying to try the cayenne pepper ones. Maybe you girls could go for a swim first, though. It's still early.'

'No,' Erica and Missy said in unison.

'I think I need a nap,' Missy added.

'And I've got a job application I was working on,' Erica put in.

Their father regarded them with a puzzled look. 'Go on then. The pool'll stay warm. I might do a few laps myself.'

'Whale in the bay!' Erica said. 'All the more reason not to go in.' Her father swatted playfully at her as she passed him on the way to the stairs.

Missy came into Erica's room with her and flopped down on the bed. 'I'm wrecked,' she said.

'Sleep, then. I'm here. I'll wake you if you get twitchy.' Erica turned on her computer. She still had to find out who Linh and Nathan had been, and now that she knew roughly how old they were it would be easier.

'Don't put any creepy music on.'

'I won't put *any* music on, how's that?'

'Fine.' Missy sounded as if she was already drifting off.

'Take your shoes off.'

Missy struggled upright and yanked at the laces of her shoes, finally toeing them off and dumping them, along with her socks, beside the bed. She curled up with her head on one of the pillows and was fast asleep within a few minutes.

Erica started her web search, tentatively at first as she wasn't sure whether the sound of the keyboard would disrupt her sister, but then getting more into it as she realised that Missy was out like a light.

Trying to find someone by their real name online was a difficult task at the best of times. So many people used online names, net nicks or handles or screen names that were different to their real names. And having only Nathan and Linh's first names and approximate ages made it harder, especially since they weren't listed in the obituaries of the *Lilywood Leader*. She got the computer looking through the classifieds of the state newspaper, and opened up a couple of webcomics in separate browser tabs to keep herself amused while the page loaded. The website was a slow one, but then it had a large database to look through, because most people who died got two or three or four obituaries, not just one.

After two hours of reading page after page of *died suddenly, dearly beloved, greatly missed*, she gave up. Maybe they'd both been from interstate. Maybe they'd both disappeared in mysterious car accidents that had taken their whole families. Maybe their families didn't even know they were dead. It didn't matter. She'd find their files at the clinic with Rose's help—she knew that the dead girl would be there when she went back. Whenever she went back. She had the feeling that she and Missy wouldn't be allowed out of their parents' sight for a long time.

She was right. Her father tapped on the door frame a few minutes later; Erica hastily closed the internet browser and swung around on her swivel chair to face him.

'I've called the radio station and told them that you won't be in for a couple of days, that you're feeling under the weather.'

'*Dad!*'

'You need some time off, Erica—can't you see how stressed you are? I'm sorry that you didn't feel like you could talk about it to us sooner, but it's obvious that something's bothering you, and if it's to do with work, then an RDO or two is just what you need.' His tone was implacable. When Richard Sayle made up his mind about something, it was not an easy thing to change that decision. In fact, Erica couldn't remember ever having successfully managed it, and he had never come home from a court case where the judge had ruled against his client.

'This isn't an RDO, Dad, it's a kidnapping. I need to work, I need the money.'

Her father shook his head and gestured around her room. 'So that you can buy more of this horror rubbish that probably set Missy off in the first place? I don't think so.'

'You don't really think that, do you?' He started to shake his head, but she overrode him. 'You do! You think that me watching a few DVDs and reading a few books screwed Missy's head up. Far out, Dad, it's not like I tied her down and made her watch with me! I even turned the volume way down or wore headphones if she asked, so she couldn't even *hear* the damn thing!' She glanced over at her sister's sleeping form and lowered her voice; she had started getting strident in her anger. 'You've got to understand, Dad, whatever triggered Missy in the first place has nothing to do with my choice of entertainment. I'd throw it all out the window right this second if I even remotely thought that.'

'I should think so. I'm not sure that you shouldn't anyway. It can't be improving her condition.'

'No, Dad. What's causing her "condition" to deteriorate is that stupid clinic.'

Her father looked hard at her and for a fleeting moment Erica wondered if he was going to hit her. He had before, although only a few times since she'd grown up—just little whacks to her shoulders or upper arms, nothing much, really. But in the end his face relaxed and went back to his standby expression of stern kindness, oxymoronic as that seemed. 'I think we've talked about it enough for the night,' he said softly.

'Yeah. We have. Especially since Missy's sleeping peacefully for the first time in months. Now that she's home again.'

Her father's face didn't change. 'I'll see you both downstairs for dinner at seven, and we can discuss what you're going to do for the next couple of days.'

'For one thing, I'm going to have to go to the doctor to get a medical certificate to explain my absence. They won't accept that I was sick without proof if it's longer than a single day,' Erica said, but it was a parting retort to her father's retreating back.

She slumped back in her chair and played Scrabble online for the next half an hour, winning one game and losing two others. Between turns she browsed real estate websites and tried to calculate how much interest she would earn if she put all of her savings in a term deposit, as opposed to leaving it in her savings account, where it was occasionally at risk if she happened to see something shiny that she wanted.

Missy woke up at some point and got out her little notebook. She liked to write poetry, although she confessed that she didn't think she was very good at it. Erica had found one of her poems once, left lying casually on the coffee table. She'd read it almost guiltily, although she was sure that Missy had left it there intentionally.

> *I look into the mirror*
> *and do not recognise the girl staring back.*
> *She has purple eye-circles,*
> *pale white skin, and a look of terror.*
> *She cannot be me—or can she?*
> *She is jumping at the shadows*
> *that move in the bathtub behind her.*
> *She is crying because she cannot escape*
> *the terrors of her own mind.*
> *She is running from darkness,*
> *but the darkness runs with her.*
> *This is not who I used to be,*
> *this is not who I want to be,*
> *this is not the person I want to see*
> *when I look into the mirror.*

She had wanted to say something to Missy about it, but in the end had just left it on the table where she had found it. She had no response to those stark, scared words. These days it seemed to be compulsory for every teenager to go through an angsty poetry-writing self-injuring (and thank God neither of them had gotten *that* bad) stage, but this wasn't just the creation of misery out of something ridiculous like a broken nail or a lost earring. This was Missy's attempt to vent off some of the jumbled dark swirl of thoughts in her brain, and to that Erica could not possibly have a solution.

They played Scrabble after dinner, crowding around the coffee table, their parents looking uncomfortable seated side by side on the battered old couch, as if the casual room was an affront to their lace doily and steam-cleaned carpet sensibilities.

It only occurred to Erica after two goes around the table that she rarely saw her parents at this end of the house; the front half was their domain, with the formal lounge and dining areas on one side of the hall and their studies on the other, and the kitchen as the halfway point where order descended into chaos, especially on nights when Missy hadn't done the dishes.

They spent time out back around the pool, sitting beside it on sun-loungers or standing next to the barbecue turning the meat carefully with tongs and taking sips from the cocktails which stood on the immaculate wooden outdoor setting. No plastic chairs and tables here. No furniture gleefully salvaged on hard rubbish collection day, as was the case in Toby's backyard (only because he and Aaron went on raids, of course), and Erica went around the pool once a week, sweeping the splashed water back in with the big black broom bought especially for that purpose.

They might have had a gardener for the back yard, someone found through Johnno the lawn bloke, except that their mother fancied that she had a green thumb and kept it nice on her own. Except for all the weeding Erica did, and all the spiky bindi-eyes that Missy picked out of the lawn between the pool and the back shed because she liked to run around out there barefoot and didn't like having spiky things embedded between her toes. She also did the watering because their mother could never remember what night they were allowed to water as the water restrictions had changed seven months ago.

It was the difference between order and chaos, the difference between the mundane and the abject, between ordinary, everyday reality and the perils of the imagination, and that was why even if Rose manifested right here in front of them and did the Nutbush on the Scrabble board, Richard Sayle would keep frowning through his glasses at the neat (alphabetised—Erica didn't peek but she knew he did it) rack of letters in front of him, and Diane Sayle would be sitting ready with the Official Scrabble Dictionary beside her on the couch, and neither of them would notice a thing.

Her father won the game. She wasn't surprised.

CHAPTER ELEVEN

At 11.29 PM, according to the softly glowing green numerals on her bedside clock, Erica's phone buzzed with a text from Toby; he was waiting outside. Erica was ready and waiting by the windowsill, and Missy was sitting on the bed, just finishing putting on her sneakers. She'd slept beside Erica—the bed was plenty big enough after all.

All that remained now was to get an explanation for why, exactly, Toby had insisted they come and meet him.

They scrambled down the rose trellis as quickly as possible.

Once they were safely out of earshot of the house—down at Toby's car, in fact, where he had parked it at the bottom of the long driveway—Erica demanded to know what was going on.

'We're going in tonight,' Toby said.

'Thanks for the warning,' Erica said.

Toby shook his head. 'If I'd told you sooner that we were going, you would have come up with all sorts of reasons not to go.'

'I don't want to hang around there at night,' Missy said.

'It'll be okay, possum, we'll be there.'

'You were there *last* time and look how well that worked out.'

Toby held up his hands. 'Peace, my darlings. We're going to have cover, remember? I've brought matches and newspaper to set off a smoke detector in the toilets, and then I'm going to pull the fire alarm. While I do that, you two will be going in whatever back door Missy can find and getting into the offices, finding whatever files you need, and getting out. Get it?'

'You're nuts,' Erica said.

'We can probably all get in through the back door into the garden,' Missy said. 'If we can get into the garden. They lock it, but one of the guys unlocks it after lights out and goes out to smoke. His room's up that end of the corridor, opposite mine. We might have to be careful that he doesn't see us.'

Erica remembered the guy she'd seen in the smoking area on her first tour. He hadn't seemed like he would notice anything unless it contained nicotine. 'Why hasn't anyone stopped him?'

'He goes out again around about five in the morning to have another smoke and he locks it again when he comes back in. I've seen him when I've been going back to bed after a treatment session.' Missy's voice was not quite steady. Erica hugged her reassuringly.

'We should probably get in this car and head out,' Toby said. 'We can talk more about the plan on the way.'

What plan? Erica wondered. It was hardly the heist of the century. It was closer to a couple of kids playing 'Ding Dong and Ditch It', except that instead of dumping flaming bags of dog poo on the front doorstep, they were going inside to hunt for evidence that would get the clinic shut down and the doctors jailed for malpractice and manslaughter and murder and whatever else the prosecution lawyers could think of.

She was willing to bet that all those friends of the Butlers, the ones who had put all the obituaries in the paper, would fork out plenty to see the clinic go down for their cover-up. It was only a shame that their father wouldn't be able to prosecute it; he had to be too involved. She had only the haziest idea of how that worked, but she was sure that Missy being a patient at the clinic made their father too close to the case.

She got in the car anyway, sitting in the back seat with Missy, making Toby comment that he felt like a chauffeur. 'Shut up and drive, Jeeves,' Missy said, sounding a little better, and she laughed when Toby laughed, which was better still.

The road was completely empty all the way to Centralia except for one solitary car going the other way with its high beams on. Toby flicked his own high beams on and off and Erica's mind automatically cross-referenced it with *Urban Legend*.

Huh. Maybe it *was* weird that she was so into all the horror stuff. Her brain insisted on tracing so many happenings in her life back to things in horror movies or books. It was lucky that Missy's didn't do the same ... or maybe it did, maybe that was part of the problem. She'd certainly seen bits of that sort of thing in their shared mindscape, but whether it had been taken from her own brain as part of the attempt to establish what scared them all, or whether Missy really *was* afraid of the things that she overheard (and oversaw? The glimpses she caught of the images on the computer screen from the doorway of Erica's room as she stood there, one foot tucked up behind her other knee, and asked for Erica to please turn the volume down?).

These thoughts kept her occupied until Toby turned off the main road onto a gravel side road, bumping and bouncing between two great old gum trees that guarded the entrance, silent sentinels with white bark gleaming in the glow of Toby's headlights.

'This isn't the way,' she said.

'I figure if we park up here we can get in over their back fence and then we're closer to the car when we want to come out again,' Toby said.

'Good planning.' She didn't relish the idea of making a run for it over the fence in the dark, but the alternative was parking at the bottom of the driveway, and that was the first place that the staff would look for a car once—if—they realised what was going on.

The side road ran up beside the Fear Clinic property and dead-ended somewhere in the general vicinity of where Erica thought the clinic's back garden would be. A chain ran across the road with a battered white-painted, rusting at the corners metal sign read

NO TRESPASSING. Beyond that it seemed to only go up to a turnaround, but maybe it went onto someone's private property. She wasn't all that concerned about where it went, though—she'd spotted a gate leading into the back garden.

'I didn't see this from the inside,' she said.

'It goes into the smoking area,' Missy said. 'They make deliveries to the kitchen through this way sometimes if it's heavy boxes. The doctors don't really like tradies traipsing through the main hallway, either.'

Toby unbuckled his seatbelt and handed out torches. Small, but powerful. 'Try not to use them if you can help it.' 'What will you be doing?'

'I'm going to go and set off the smoke alarm in the men's toilets just off the kitchen, hit the fire alarm switch, and hope like hell that you two can get inside and to the offices in the confusion.'

'But we've got to go past the kitchen to get in,' Missy said.

'Crap. True. Damn.'

'Why don't we see if we can get into the garden first,' Erica said, 'and then worry about exactly how to go inside?' Something was niggling at her brain, something about the rec room ... something relevant. Maybe.

'Okay.' Toby handed her a green fabric shopping bag. 'I brought this for you to carry the papers in when you find them.' Erica folded it flat and slipped it inside her t-shirt, and then got out of the car, shutting the door as quietly as she could manage.

The gate was locked, and Erica wasn't too keen on the idea of climbing over it and jumping down onto the pavers. They sidled along the wall towards the far end of the garden. It was shadowy—no, more than shadowy. The *shadows* had shadows. Erica kept expecting one of them to open a mouth bristling with fangs and bite her head off. She glanced at Missy every two seconds, but Missy was fine. The prospect of unmasking the doctors had given her a new burst of enthusiasm, and she was the first over the wall when at last they found a conveniently placed tree, swinging up into it with a display of the dexterity she had picked up through her years of gymnastics, and balancing lightly atop the wall before rappelling down the ivy on the other side. Erica followed her, needing a boost up to the first branch from Toby, who jumped up and caught it himself when it was his turn. At last they were all standing at the end of the garden, looking at the back wall of the clinic.

'I think we need to get a bit closer,' Erica whispered. 'I can't see the doors.' And that was when she remembered what it was she was supposed to remember about the rec room. There was a door in there marked STAFF ONLY, and she would bet her complete collection of Stephen King novels that it led back down that side of the building to the offices. 'Missy, follow me when we get inside.'

'Where were you planning to go?'

'Just do it, okay? Toby, I need you to make as noisy a diversion as you can and then either get out or come and find us.'

'Be careful,' Missy said. 'They could be anywhere.'

They moved along the wall towards the back door, only stepping away from its cover when they reached the second wall that marked the edge of the smoking area. A security light snapped on and the three of them froze. Footsteps came close to the back door. A cat darted across the lawn, and the footsteps went away again. Toby reached up and twisted the security light out of its socket so that they wouldn't set it off again. He listened at the door, crouching low, pretending to be just a bush that had wandered out of the garden. Then he tried the knob. The door was open, swinging smoothly inward when he pushed it. He moved inside and disappeared through the archway that led to the kitchen and dining area.

Erica led Missy inside and they turned right into the rec room, crossing the floor in a crouched, shambling scuttle, stopping behind a chair that would block any view of them from the doorway and was close to the STAFF ONLY door. Gesturing for Missy to stay put, Erica crawled the last two metres and tried the knob. Locked. She wasn't surprised. She also didn't think that it would be a terribly strong lock; the staff doubtless relied on trust in their patients and the big sign on the door to respect their privacy. Given how completely her privacy had been violated, she was going to kick their stupid door in with no compunctions whatsoever. But she had to wait until Toby was making enough noise.

It took an agonisingly long time before first the smoke alarm and then the fire alarm went off. As soon as they did Erica leapt to her feet and kicked the door as close to the handle as she could manage. The lock popped open and she ran through, beckoning Missy after her. The door wouldn't close properly behind them but that was all right; they'd need to get out quickly.

They were in a long corridor, not as wide as the main hallway. They had to go single file, and Erica wondered what would happen if two people needed to pass each other. There was a series of numbered doors that doubtless led to the corresponding treatment rooms—or more specifically, the viewing rooms behind the one-way glass—and after a while, another closed door that opened when Erica tried the handle. They were on familiar territory now; she could see Doctor Chapman's office.

Both of them could hear the pandemonium going on beyond the door out to the reception area. Running feet, people shouting, and someone wailing in a constant rising and falling tone that sounded like an ambulance siren. And over it all, the piercing shriek of the fire alarm and the beep-beep-beep of multiple smoke detectors.

Missy sniffed. 'Can you smell that?' she asked. 'I think something really *is* on fire.'

'Stupid idiot,' Erica said. 'He's really done it. We'd better hurry.' She opened the office door, which had been locked until she put her elbow through the window glass and unlocked it from the inside, and went in. Missy followed her and shut the door, and then pulled the roller blind down over it to hide the broken glass.

'Lucky this isn't a proper psych hospital. Their glass is probably a lot stronger,' she murmured.

Erica stifled a snort. 'Not to mention that they probably don't take too well to the idea of patients sneaking out of the back door at night for a smoke.'

'Come on, let's get on with it,' Missy said. She switched on her torch and shone it around the room. 'There's a filing cabinet.'

Erica slid the top drawer open and found patient files, sorted A to E by surname. BUTLER, ROSE wasn't in there, though.

'She's not here,' she said. She flipped through again, but BUTLER, ROSE was still nowhere to be found.

'Try the other drawers,' Missy suggested. She was looking around the office, her torchlight dancing across a hanging plant and the desk and the chair and a coat rack. 'Oh, hey ...'

'Oh, hey, what?' Erica pulled open the next drawer down and flicked through the files. No BUTLER, ROSE. No files with NATHAN or LINH as a first name, either. She tried the third drawer, getting rapidly frustrated.

'There's another door here.' Erica heard the door open. 'Stairs.'

'Stairs?'

'Basement stairs,' Missy clarified.

'Let's go,' Erica said, shutting the drawers and hurrying to join her sister. The stairs were steep and narrow and wooden, and their steps made jarringly loud sounds as they descended.

It didn't help that Rose materialised just as Erica was reaching out to open the door at the bottom, so that Erica put a hand halfway into Rose's chest.

'Careful,' Rose complained.

'Sorry.' Rose moved aside, and Erica opened the door.

The room on the other side was the autopsy room from the mindscape. At least now they knew where to go.

Erica charged straight across the room to the desk, took a good look at the three manila folders to make certain that they were the correct ones (BUTLER, ROSE; WARD, NATHAN; and TRUONG, LINH), and then shoved them into her green bag, putting it back inside her t-shirt and tucking her t-shirt securely into her jeans, then pulling her jumper down over it all. The exercise only took about two minutes, all told.

'Hide!' Rose said from the doorway, and Erica and Missy dove for the kneehole under the desk, realising they wouldn't both fit, and then squeezing in anyway as footsteps came clattering down the stairs.

'Dale? Dale! Are you down here? I've got one of them,' Doctor Chapman called out as she came into the room. She had Toby; his arm was twisted up behind his back and there was soot and dirt all over his face. Doubtless there was a story behind that, but Erica wasn't about to step out and ask. Toby saw her, but flicked his eyes away so that Doctor Chapman wouldn't notice. 'Dale!'

'I'm here, I'm here,' came the reply from the other room beyond the archway. Doctor Morley came out into the autopsy room, looking harried. 'What on earth is going on?'

'I found this one in one of the bedrooms trying to burn the place down,' Doctor Chapman said, shaking Toby roughly. His head was lolling to one side a bit, and Erica wondered if he'd been drugged again.

Doctor Morley looked up at the ceiling. 'It sounds rather as if he succeeded,' he said dryly.

'The orderlies can take care of it,' Doctor Chapman said. 'We need to find somewhere to store this one and find the other two.'

'Other two?'

'Dale, don't you listen to anything I tell you? This one was in here earlier today with the Sayle girl and her sister.' Doctor Chapman sighed. 'At the very least you should have noticed the additional output from room twelve this afternoon.'

'I did see that, yes,' Doctor Morley said. 'I assumed you'd simply taken the Sayle girl to the next level of treatment.'

'And you didn't bother to check the monitor to make certain that everything was going well, despite the energy level trebling. Congratulations, Dale. You're officially obsessed with your work.' Doctor Chapman moved forward, hustling Toby in front of her. She went past the desk and through the archway into the next room. 'You might as well have this one. Coulrophobia, but it might be masks in general. He's very strong mentally, but once he breaks, he's well and truly productive.'

'What were the other two?'

'The Sayle source was nycto, but more specifically she was afraid that something would come out of the darkness and attack her. No history of abuse to trigger it, oddly enough, or at least she says not.' Missy's hands balled into fists at the implication.

'Pity. Specific incidents are stronger.'

'Her sister was harder to place, but there was some reaction to the drowning sequence, and to the spider in the circus scene, although I'm fairly certain that the reaction there was due to her helplessness. She likes to be in control, that one.' Doctor Chapman chuckled. It was not a pleasant sound. 'I'm going to go and round up the troops. Keep yourself amused. I'll be back later.' There was a thump from the inner room and then Doctor Chapman came striding back out, went up the stairs, and disappeared without looking back.

Erica could hear Doctor Morley humming in the inner room, and scrambled out from underneath the desk as quietly as she could. Her legs had started to cramp up. Missy crawled out as well and stretched hugely.

'Now what?' she whispered, her lips against Erica's ear.

Erica looked around the room. There was a tray of autopsy tools beside the autopsy table. The bone saw was electric, but that didn't matter; it didn't need to be plugged in for her to hit someone with it.

'Erica, what are you doing?'

'Getting Toby back.'

The room beyond the archway was instantly familiar from dozens of *X-Files* episodes: it was a morgue, but a bizarre one. Stainless steel drawers lined one wall. Another door at the other end of the room stood open; the room beyond it glowed with a soft blue light. A large cluster of computer cables ran into the morgue from the ceiling, gathered together in one corner, and passed through a slot beside the open door. A soft electrical humming sound came from the other side of the doorway.

Doctor Morley had his back to her, fussing over something in front of him. Erica moved up behind him as quietly as she could manage and then swung the solid bone saw sideways at his temple. He heard her, and began to turn around, but she caught the side of his head anyway and he crumpled to the floor, his glasses falling off on the way down.

He had been strapping Toby into a chair. Toby was fading fast, but wasn't so far gone that he couldn't get up when she unstrapped him. A set of the VR goggles were on a tray attached to the arm of the chair, along with a pair of the gloves. Struggling a little, Erica got Doctor Morley into the chair and put the VR goggles and gloves on him. She had no idea how to switch the machine on, though there was a blue switch on the chair that looked promising. It would help to disorient him. She strapped him in and left him there. He was already groaning a little, beginning to come around. There was a nasty red bump where she'd clocked him with the bone saw.

'We need to get out of here,' Toby said muzzily. 'I think the bed was on fire.'

'What the hell did you do, Toby?' Erica asked.

'Missy's room was still vacant so I went in there and set the sheets alight so there would be something for them to find, not just an alarm for no reason. But one of the guys grabbed me and then Chapman came and poked me with her needle again.' He yawned. 'Hope none of them was pyrophobic ...'

Erica thought of the rising and falling wail she had heard, and said, 'I think at least one of them was.'

'Oh. Hell. Well, now they've got a good reason for it.'

'There're fire extinguishers all over the place up there. How come I can still smell smoke?' Missy asked.

'Never mind that now. Let's go.'

'You're not going anywhere,' Doctor Chapman said from the doorway. 'Not a chance.' She was backed up by four orderlies, big men who looked fully prepared to break a few limbs if that was what it took to keep the trio in one place.

Erica pulled the hammer back out of her belt loop and lifted it in one hand. It felt pathetically inadequate against the hulking wall of force behind Doctor Chapman. 'Just try us,' she said, knowing that they would, and that she would fail, and that the water-dream and the dark cavern were waiting on the other side of the VR goggles.

The orderlies started forward. Toby and Missy were already moving towards the blue-glowing doorway. Erica took half a second to flip the blue switch set into the side of the strap-chair's headrest, and then bolted after them as Doctor Morley began screaming in a thin voice. The electrical humming sound grew louder, but Erica barely noticed it, focussed as she was on getting into the next room. She had little hope of there being a way out through the doorway, but there might be a better weapon than a little rubber hammer.

'Don't let them go through that door!' Doctor Chapman hollered. 'There's valuable scientific equipment in there that can't be disturbed!'

Erica felt the brush of a hand on her shoulder and dove through the doorway.

The world disappeared.

Chapter Twelve

She was standing with Toby and Missy on what looked like a huge factory floor. The predominant feature of the place was the hundreds—no, thousands—of wires that ran into the room from thousands of holes in the walls, making the walls look like gigantic circuit boards.

As they ran down the walls some of the wires were spliced together into larger wires; others were split and became finer. They were all coated in coloured—colour-coded?—plastic. They ran into a series of large upright metal boxes that hummed and hummed with power. The metal boxes were connected with the thickest wires of all, each one about as thick around as Erica's upper arm. These wires first connected the boxes and then ran across the floor at the far end of the factory into a long bank of computers, which were beeping away industriously—rows of figures scrolled up their screens, each one different. The far wall was glass with a door in it, leading through to another room where Erica could just see another set of computers. The place was maybe three hundred feet long and half as wide, and the ceiling was maybe fifty feet up.

The floor beneath their feet was cement, but well kept, smoothly polished, and coloured a warm orange that let a homely feel to the bizarre space. The walls were barely visible under the snake nest of wires, but the parts that Erica could see were painted deep blue, like the sky at noon in high summer. Turning around, the door that they had entered through wasn't there any more—in fact, she couldn't tell how they had gotten in, because the wall was just like all the others.

'What the hell?' Toby said.

'We're not in the mindscape again, are we?' Erica asked, touching her front to reassure herself that the files were still tucked in under her t-shirt.

'I don't think so,' Missy said. 'This is weird, but not scary. But it's *very* weird.' She was turning in a slow circle, looking around. 'Check out the ceiling.'

Erica looked up. The ceiling was divided into two fairly distinct parts. The section closest to them was painted the same bright blue as the walls. In the centre of this section a cheerful yellow sun beamed down at them—it wore sunglasses and had a big grin painted on it, and was surrounded by eight triangles, alternating orange and red, presumably intended to represent its rays. Light came from the sun, although how it did, Erica wasn't sure—there wasn't a visible light bulb, but maybe it was one big flat bulb and she just couldn't tell because it was so far above her head.

'Real?' she asked Missy. 'Not real?'

'I ... don't know.' Missy was on her third or fourth circle. 'At the start of the simulations, the virtual reality usually takes a minute to become fully immersive. This doesn't feel like that does.'

There was a blurry area in the centre of the ceiling where the blue darkened to purple, with streaks of pink and red mixed in. Then the purple darkened to black, dotted with white blobs that were probably meant to be stars. A big round full moon was painted in silver in the middle of this section, and again it was somehow emitting light, as were the stars—tiny pinpricks of light from this far below them. Erica could imagine someone up there, lying on their back on a plank set across two ladders, painting away with the paint dripping down onto them.

'It's so pretty,' she said.

'I'm glad you think so!' said a voice from the far end of the room. Erica looked to see two young women standing there, near the bank of computers. They were both smiling. 'We work hard to make the place look nice.' The one who was speaking patted the potted palm that was next to the computer bank. 'It's hard when there's so much technology.' She sounded apologetic.

'It's very nice,' Toby said. 'Where, um, is it, exactly?'

The other girl frowned. 'There isn't any *exact*, to be honest. It just *is*. We've never thought to try and be exact about it. It's everywhere.'

'It can't be *everywhere*,' Toby said. He was frowning as well, puzzled, seeking certainty.

'All right. Some of it, the places where the wires come in, is everywhere, and the bit you're standing on is *here*. Is that better?' The first girl grinned.

'It's a marginal improvement.' Toby looked like he wouldn't be happy until he had notes on latitude and longitude.

'Well, don't just stand there, come on up here and we'll give you the tour. You did come for the tour, right?' the second girl asked.

Erica, Toby, and Missy exchanged a glance. 'Not exactly,' Erica said cautiously.

'No? Oh well, we can show you around anyway and worry about why you're here later.' The first girl was clearly happy to have visitors. She had long brown hair in two pigtails and was wearing a lab coat decorated with colourful swirls over a white polo shirt and black jeans. The second girl had left her lab coat unadorned but there were several pens poking out of its pocket, and the rest of her outfit was the same as the first girl's. She had short blonde hair, ruffled up into spikes, with a few blue streaks running through it.

'Okay, sure,' Erica said. 'I'm Erica. This is Toby and Missy.' She might as well go along with the scene. If she could do that, then maybe she could anticipate the bad stuff when it happened.

'Oh, we know who *you* are,' the first girl said. 'After yesterday afternoon—whew! You nearly blew the circuits with all that energy!' She grinned again. 'Just kidding. It would take more than three people to blow the circuits. I'm Polly at the moment, and this is—Cleo, I think, with that hair.'

'This conversation would be a lot easier if we weren't bellowing it from opposite ends of the factory,' Cleo said, clearly unimpressed. She started walking towards the trio, and as she moved her appearance seemed to change, running through a number of different visages, male and female and neither and both, with different skin colours and hair colours and clothes and heights and sizes, before fixing itself back to the way they had first seen her when she stopped walking, about six feet away. Polly, after pouring a little water onto the potted palm out of a plastic watering can, trotted after her, going through a similar dizzying sequence of changes before she stopped in front of them.

'What the hell was that?' Erica asked.

'We're having a little trouble with integrity at the moment,' Polly explained. 'I think it's interference from the machines. It just takes a little focus to stay in one shape.'

'What *are* you?' Toby asked.

'Oh, we get called programmers—well, we get called a lot of things, but that's what we get called *here*—but really the computers do all the work and we just push a few buttons. But I'm getting ahead of myself.' Polly laughed an embarrassed little laugh. 'I do that a lot. Cleo, do you want to start?'

Cleo looked more like she wanted to sidle off to a corner and pretend she didn't exist. 'These boxes're the collection modules,' she said, tapping one of them—it went *dong, dong* when she did so. 'They receive the input, which is then converted to code and channelled to the computers, where it's matched with the most suitable recipient. Kind of like a blood bank sorting by blood type, except that instead of A and B and O you've got your horror, your fantasy, your romance, that sort of thing. See?'

'No,' Erica, Missy, and Toby said in unison.

'That's hardly explaining it from the *start*, Cleo,' Polly said in a mock severe tone. 'It all begins with the input. Now that can come in from a number of sources. As you might know, you were part of the fear input, via the VR machines at the clinic. The electrical energy of your fear gets drawn out—it's amazing how much you can do with brainwaves when you know how!—and comes to us via the clinic input, which is the blue wires.'

She pointed to an apparently random section of the wall. Erica looked and saw what appeared to be a tangle of standard network cables—like the wires she had seen going through the slot beside the door. They ran down the wall, were spliced together at one point, and disappeared into one of the humming boxes.

'The energy gets mixed up with energy from the other sources and then they all get channelled to their particular primary computer—in your case, to the horror processor. It reassembles the energy into ideas that are a reworking or in some cases just a slight alteration of whatever it was that scared you.

Sometimes it doesn't need to make any changes, because of course there are some things that scare enough people that they don't need to be made more accessible—and then passes it on to the secondary computers.'

'Which is where we come in,' Cleo broke in, looking a lot more animated. 'We run the program to match the ideas, or the plot seeds, or whatever you like to call them, to a recipient. Sometimes it's someone more well-known, but just by way of an example, we wouldn't give Toby's cannibal clowns experience to Stephen King, because chances are that's where it came from in the first place. But the computer would rework it, make it more original and less susceptible to all those little things like plagiarism accusations and copyright issues, and shoot it off to someone who can put their own twist on it. With the giant spider thing and that bloody tiger—I loved that, by the way, very gory—it becomes something a little different, maybe the basis for a scene in a book dealing with phobias or something like that. Something like that, we'd send off to a writer who's got a bit of a plot formed but needs to flesh it out with a few graphic scenes.' She gestured to the far wall. 'So we're at the computers in there, and once it looks like we've got a finalised seed, we fire it off and hope it hits.'

'I suppose you're wondering how we target it,' Polly said. 'With the big names—take Stephen King, for example—we can usually target their specific geographical area to within a few miles. It's funny reading about him going on his walks to try and fire up his brain, because we know that that means if we misfired, he'll pick it up sooner or later. Of course it's terribly hard to get anywhere close with some people. And if we don't have a specific target we have to try and find someone who's receptive to the idea and can make something of it, because otherwise it's a waste of an idea—one of those ones that ends up as an unfinished trunk novel or doesn't even get *outlined*, which makes me *spit* considering how hard we work here.' She grabbed Erica's arm. 'Come and we'll show you that end of it.'

Erica stared at her, not moving. 'You mean ... no. You don't give writers ideas, do you?'

'Got it in one,' Cleo said. 'Whenever a writer gets asked the question, "Where do you get your ideas?", they usually have some answer about a pipe into the subconscious or a pool of ideas or subverting common tropes. But the real answer is that it's here. We do it. All of it. And it's hard work.'

'It can't possibly work,' Toby said. 'This is insane.' Yet he stared around in awe now instead of in confusion, and when Cleo slipped her hand into the crook of his arm, leading him towards the bank of computers, he went unresistingly. Missy was already there, peering intently at one of the screens.

'It makes no sense,' she called back.

'That's just the coding part,' Polly said. 'The electrical impulses have to be converted into a form that the secondary computers can make into a logical sequence, otherwise the whole thing goes utterly *haywire* and things get written that perhaps shouldn't have.'

Polly put a hand on Cleo's shoulder. 'Stress less, honey,' she said. 'We do what we could to fix it.' In an aside to the trio, she added, 'Cleo's taste in books leans towards those that don't have random punctuation in their character names.'

'I guess everyone has their own personal preferences,' Missy said.

'Yeah, well, I'd *prefer* to stick my head in a blender than see another gratuitous apostrophe,' Cleo muttered.

'Play nice,' Polly said squeezing Cleo's shoulder and then stepping away. 'Don't forget all our achievements.'

'Let's just go look at the fun stuff, okay?' Cleo, stiff-backed and bristly-haired, led them through to the room behind the glass wall. There were a number of computers here but only two of them were actively running. As they entered the room, one of them let out a soft chime.

'Oh!' Polly said. 'Good timing! We've got one ready.'

Cleo hurried to the computer and dropped into the chair in front of it, fingers flying across the keyboard. Erica, certain that this was just another virtual reality experience, went and stood behind her nonetheless, watching the screen. Toby and Missy joined her, squeezing in together to all be able to see the monitor.

It was difficult to say just what was happening on the monitor. One moment it was a series of words scrolling up the screen, the next a flickering series of images, the next an eye-bending *something* that appeared to be, for lack of any other explanation, a visual representation of the feeling of terror when something came out of the dark and grabbed you. Missy certainly jumped back when it appeared as if she recognised it, and Polly put a steadying hand on her back.

'Sorry, hon. That's one of yours. I didn't realise. The computer's not always that quick to assimilate the data.'

'Where's it going?' Missy asked.

'We don't know just yet,' Cleo answered, still typing away. 'That's what I'm doing now—checking it against the databases to see if there's anyone it would fit best with.' The computer chimed again and she let out a satisfied, 'Ahhhh.' A map of the world flashed up on the monitor and simultaneously on a much larger screen on one wall. 'Target acquired.'

'So where's it going?' Missy asked again.

'Looks like Australia,' Polly said. The map wasn't exactly a standard geopolitical portrayal; it had areas marked out in various colours that matched the wires on the wall, and this was overlaid by a network of lines and dots. One of the dots was blinking. 'Yep, Australia.' She went over to the map and touched a button on the wall beside it, and a set of coordinates appeared beside the dot.

'Locked in,' Cleo said. She got up and crossed to the other side of the room, where a strange contraption awaited. It was like a chair, but with a large attachment sprouting up almost organically from one arm that looked like a gunsight. A thick cable ran from the computer hub to the machine on the chair. Cleo slipped into the chair, set her feet on the pedals—like a brake and accelerator—and closed her hands around the handles, yanking them towards herself with a muffled obscenity. 'Someone else used it and didn't put it back the way it was,' she explained, with a pointed glare at Polly.

'You're not the only one who gets to use it,' Polly said gently.

Cleo just tightened her grip on the handles and pulled the sight down so she could peer into it. The tube poked out through a hole in the outer wall, but Erica couldn't see what lay beyond that wall—it was just black, not the black of darkness, but the black of nothingness, of waiting, of the time before the beginning.

Polly laughed and Erica realised she'd spoken aloud. 'Very close,' she said. 'Very close indeed.'

'Whenever you're ready, this thing would work better with the correct coordinates,' Cleo griped.

'Sorry,' Polly said. She went over to Cleo's computer and pressed a round green button on the keyboard. The computer beeped and the screen went black, and then the words FILE COMPLETED appeared briefly before the computer double-beeped and went back to running the matching program.

Cleo pressed down on the right pedal with her foot and thumbed a green button on the left-hand-side handle, whispering, 'Pow!' as she did so. 'And that's it,' she said, sitting back in the chair and smiling. 'Of course, occasionally it misses, but it usually gets within a few miles.'

'Modesty,' Polly said. 'Cleo hasn't missed by more than five feet since she started. And with something that close, the intended recipient usually picks the idea up within a few hours—days at the outside, unless they're somewhere they don't usually go.'

'What if they don't find it at all?' Erica asked.

'Sometimes a family member or a friend gets it instead and then we just have to hope that they're not a bad writer. Mind you, that's how a lot of bad stories get written. We miss.' Cleo got up and pushed a yellow button on the side of the contraption. 'Even so, it's all good practice. It's not like anyone's made a required reading list for the whole world, anyway.'

'I wouldn't read it,' Erica said, and Cleo snickered.

'Now that you've seen the place, let's go and sit in the tearoom and have a cuppa and you can tell us what you're doing here,' Polly said. 'It's unusual for people to come here and not know where they are, or why they're here.'

'Let's do that,' Toby said. 'And while we're at it, you can explain how this whole place can possibly be run by just two people and a bunch of computers.'

Polly laughed. 'For starters, it's hardly just the two of us. No ideas would get anywhere if it rested in the hands of just two people. But that's a fair point. I need an Iced Vo-Vo before I explain anything like that though. It gets a bit complicated. Possibly even a lot complicated, if we have to start from the beginning.'

'Yeah!' Missy said. 'How does a place like this even exist?'

'Well, come on and we'll talk about it,' Polly said. Cleo had already walked through a door near the large screen on the left-hand wall, and the sound of coffee percolating clearly had Polly's attention.

Erica hung back, grabbing Toby's sleeve, as Polly and Missy went into the tearoom. 'What the hell *is* this?' she hissed. 'We've got to be in the mindscape again. This can't be *real*.'

'If it's the mindscape, where's the darkness? Why isn't the room filling with water, or a big old tsunami of clowns flooding the whole joint? This isn't scary, it's *incredible*.' Toby pulled away. 'Even if this *is* the mindscape, this is interesting, and we might as well play along.'

'Fine,' Erica said. 'But the minute one of these two starts doing anything creepy, I'm going to brain them.' She held up the bone saw. 'There's no way I'm going through anything like that again.'

'If some outside force is controlling this, then you won't have a choice.'

'If some outside force is controlling this and the same garbage goes down as before, I am going to put this thing through its *eye*,' Erica said, and followed Toby into the tearoom.

She felt a bit silly after her little speech when the tearoom turned out to be as mundane as the one at work. Two long tables with benches ran down the middle of the room, there was a workbench along two of the walls with an inbuilt dishwasher and oven, and the coffee machine on the bench was state of the art. Polly and Missy were sitting at one end of one table, and Cleo was pouring out the coffee.

'Coffee? Tea? Cocoa?' she asked.

'Tea,' Toby said.

'Just water, thanks,' Erica said. Tap water she could see through. Tap water was less likely to have drugs in it. Sort of. She didn't like the way that Cleo raised an eyebrow at her before filling the glass, but that wasn't enough to attack her over.

They settled around the table with their mugs (and Erica's glass) and Cleo brought over the biscuit tin. Once they each had a biscuit (Erica abstained for about three seconds but then succumbed to the call of the Tim Tams), Polly looked around at them.

'So, how exactly did you get here?' she asked.

'From the Fear Clinic in Centralia,' Erica said. 'We were on the basement level looking for evidence that Rose died at the clinic, and Doctor Morley grabbed Toby, and I knocked him out, but then Doctor Chapman showed up and the only place we could go was through the blue door.'

Polly and Cleo looked at each other, and then back at Erica. 'Who is Rose?' Cleo asked.

'You mean you don't know? I thought you'd know. You knew *us*,' Erica said.

'We knew you because of the power surge,' Cleo said. 'We don't usually know individual names, just the locations of the input centres.'

'Well, Rose died in your stupid "input centre",' Missy said, 'so you *should* know her name. She died, and they covered it up, and two other people as well.'

'How did she die?' Polly asked, her bouncy demeanour gone, a serious look on her face as she leaned across the table, hands clasped around her coffee mug, her Iced Vo-Vo lying forgotten in front of her.

'We think it was a brain haemorrhage,' Erica said. 'But they burned her body, so there's no proof there.' She remembered the files and pulled them out of her t-shirt, spreading them out on the table. 'Hopefully these are evidence.'

'Who's "they" who covered it up?' Cleo asked.

'The doctors,' Toby said.

Cleo let out a long sigh and dropped her head onto the table, banging it gently against the wood. 'I was afraid of this,' she said in a muffled voice. Polly put an arm around her. Cleo lifted her head again. 'I *knew* this would happen. It keeps happening with the romance section—they fall in love and then don't want to do their job because they're too busy having sex—and now the fear collectors are getting into it as well. They're not *in* a horror novel, they need to focus on their job, and this means bringing them back here and finding someone else to cover for them while we *fix* them.'

'We can turn it over to the personnel department,' Polly said, 'but Cleo's right, it's not good enough. When we get to spend time in the physical world it's a privilege, not a right, and they've violated the rules by not stopping the project as soon as someone died.' She looked at Missy. 'You said there were two others as well?'

'Nathan Ward and Linh Truong,' Missy said, tapping the folders.

'Nathan ... no.' Cleo had her Teddy Bear biscuit in her hand; her hand reflexively tightened at the sound of Nathan's name, and the biscuit fell to the table, reduced to crumbs. 'He was one of the first test subjects,' she said bitterly. 'Fiona found him living in a box behind Coles in Centralia, shaking in fear every time he heard something moving in the rubbish because it might be a rat. He was petrified of them. A perfect first subject. He was getting better though. The idea of the Fear Clinic was to siphon people's irrational fear off. Make them better, make them able to cope. Not kill them.'

'According to this, he killed himself,' Erica said, reading the front page of Nathan's file. 'He broke a water glass and cut his wrists in his bathroom, forty-five minutes after his last treatment session. They found him before he died, but he'd lost too much blood.' She turned a page. 'He was only semiconscious, but told the orderly who found him that "they came out of the mattress and bit me so I ran and they won't get me now".' She closed the file. 'That was six months ago and you're telling us you didn't know about it?'

'We knew his treatment program had ended,' Cleo said. 'We assumed it had been successful.'

'And what, that he'd been sent back home to his nice cardboard box?' Toby snapped. 'You don't care where the ideas come from as long as they keep coming, right?'

'That's not true!' Polly said, anguished. 'Fiona—Doctor Chapman—told us that his program had ended and that he was no longer phobic.'

'Yeah, well, that's true, isn't it? He's dead. I doubt he's afraid of *anything* now.'

'Toby, stop it,' Erica said. 'They didn't know. I don't think they communicate that closely with the real world.' She looked at Polly and Cleo; Polly was rubbing Cleo's back, probably as much for her own comfort as for Cleo's. 'Nathan killed himself. Rose had a brain haemorrhage. And according to this—' she flipped open Linh's file '—Linh had a heart attack. Oh, and she was acrophobic, by the way. Three perfectly normal people with three perfectly common phobias, and all three died, and your doctors covered it up. The issue here isn't that you should have known. The question is, what are you going to do about it now?'

'We need to bring Fiona and Dale through and fix them,' Cleo said. She lifted her hand and began brushing the biscuit crumbs off it. 'They're just like us, you know. But when we—when we go out into the world, we don't always cope very well. It's hard to adjust. Our reactions get exaggerated; our emotions are stronger than yours simply because we're getting to express them out there instead of in here, where we all already know how we all think.'

'So someone else will go and replace them? Won't that look a bit suspicious?' Erica asked.

'I've never heard of a hospital only having two doctors, even one as specialised as this. Their replacements—and I'm thinking that Nikola and Rupinder would be good—will simply explain that the doctors are out of town at a medical conference and will be back soon. It will only take a few days of your time, after all.'

'And then what, the clinic keeps going? After all that's happened?'

'You don't understand,' said Polly. 'We can change them so that it doesn't happen again. They won't want to give in to the fear and be a part of the cause. The only people they will take fear from is the people who've checked into the clinic voluntarily, and they'll complete the program the way it was intended to be completed. We only want to take what's there already to help people, not induce more than they can stand just to run the machines.'

'I just don't know how they got so out of control without Personnel noticing,' Cleo said. 'They're supposed to be monitoring this closely, making sure it doesn't happen. They're always right on the ball with the romance idiots, and even when Dean—was it Dean?—got all tangled up with that guy who thought he was Gandalf, they were right on that before anybody got a magical staff stuck anywhere, so why is this different?'

'Apart from anything else, it's *working*,' Toby said. 'You said it yourself, we tripled the input for the machine, but only because the doctors did the wrong thing. If that's the case—and if keeping people there longer than necessary also increases production—then what's a few deaths in the grand scheme of things? People die when they go to war, but one side or the other always claims to be the winners, even when thousands of people don't live to see the victory.'

'God, Toby, stop it,' Erica said.

'Why should I? *They* didn't.' He got up abruptly, almost falling backwards off the bench as he scooted out, and stormed out into the main factory floor. Erica could hear him stomping around out there and the occasional hollow clang as he kicked one of the boxes.

'He can't break them,' Cleo said.

'I wasn't all that worried, to be honest,' Erica said, glaring at her.

'We need to recall Fiona and Dale and send Nikola and Rupinder in, if they're them at the moment.' Polly got up and put the lid back on the biscuit tin, replacing it on the bench next to the coffee machine, and swept Cleo's biscuit crumbs up with a little dustpan and brush, tipping them into the bin.

'Rupinder's always being someone else,' Cleo said.

'If you're sick of being Cleo, change,' Polly snapped. '*I'm* sick of hearing you whine, no matter who you're being, so if you're going to change, pick someone who's got a better attitude.'

The whole situation was already surreal, but was getting odder by the second. Cleo's face shimmered and shifted for almost a minute, but then her features stabilised. Erica and Missy watched in silence so complete it seemed that the other two had forgotten they were there, as Polly stared Cleo down.

'I'll be Cleo,' Cleo said at last. 'Cleo's got *you*.' And she held her arms up for Polly to come over and embrace her. They held each other for a long moment, and then apparently remembered that Erica and Missy were still sitting there.

'It's a long story,' Polly said.

'I think we've established that it's not just a long story, it's some sort of fantasy epic,' Erica said. 'Get Toby back in here, he can write it all down.'

'Leave him be,' Cleo said. 'He's in an awful mood, and I can understand that. Unfortunately, we're running an ideas machine here, not a time machine. We can't go back and save Nathan or Rose or Linh, so we're going to do the best that we can with what we've got to prevent anything else happening at the clinic.'

'Couldn't you just shut the clinic down?' Missy asked.

'No,' Polly said after a thoughtful pause. 'It's a good idea in theory, but no matter whatever else is going on because Dale and Fiona stopped doing their job properly, people are coming out of there healthy and alive with their phobias cured. Even yours can be fixed once we get things back up and running smoothly.'

'There's not a chance in hell that I'm going to let that VR crap anywhere near me,' Missy snapped, and for a second the confidence she had been displaying thus far vanished, showing how pale her face was, how scared her eyes. 'I'd rather go back to the early nineteen hundreds and get a lobotomy.'

'Yuck, Missy, don't say that,' Erica said. 'That's barbaric.'

'And inducing a fear reaction in someone so bad that they blow a fuse in their brain isn't? Jesus. Come on, then, let's go see whoever you guys have gotta see to get this fixed.' Missy pointed at the other door leading out of the tearoom. 'Through there, right?'

'No, that's just our sleeping quarters,' Polly said, looking defeated. 'This way.' They went back through the glassed-in computer room; Toby joined them as they reached the door on the other side, which was marked EXECUTIVE OFFICES. Erica half expected it to say NO TRESPASSING underneath, but it didn't.

Polly stopped before opening the door. 'Actually, maybe you'd better stay here,' she said. 'Considering you came here by accident, it might be a better idea if you didn't see *everything*.'

Erica held up the files. 'We're making sure these get seen by the right eyes,' she said. 'In person.'

Polly nodded, as if she'd expected the response, and opened the door.

The area on the other side was carpeted in the same warm orange colour as the factory floor. The whole place seemed to be designed for maximum comfort, and small wonder if these people worked so hard at such an important job. The walls were blue, the ceiling was white with grey lines on it indicating the edges of clouds, and everything was as open as possible. It was a central area with a couple of coffee tables and couches in the very middle (the couches were upholstered in an eye-burning clash of blue, orange, and red, Erica was pleased to note—not cream), and several open doors leading off it. She saw a door marked REHABILITATION and a door marked TOILETS and a door marked PERSONNEL, which Polly walked determinedly towards. Having decided to let the trio in, she had clearly made up her mind to get it over and done with. Erica glanced through the REHABILITATION door as she walked past it, but saw only a room that looked like an ordinary psychiatrist's office. She had seen a couple of those in the search for a cure for Missy.

Polly tapped on the PERSONNEL door and a deep, agreeable voice said, 'Come in.'

'It's me, sir, Polly, and Cleo, and some visitors.' Polly stood aside to let the others through. Cleo went in first with Erica close on her heels—if this new person posed any danger she wanted to be ready for it and have Missy safely out of the way.

He was a black man with hair cropped close to his head, wearing a soft grey shirt and black trousers. He sat behind a desk that was dwarfed by his tall frame, and his smile when he saw Erica was open and welcoming. 'We don't often get visitors to our humble company,' he said, and his voice was rich and smooth.

'It's a nice place, sir,' Erica said.

'Come now, I know you don't know my name, but Polly and Cleo certainly do, and "sir" isn't necessary. I'm Jon.' He extended a hand across the desk. 'And you are?'

'Erica. Erica Sayle. This is my sister Missy, and my friend Toby Noonan.' His grip was warm and gentle. 'Pleased to meet you.'

'Likewise. It's always good to have visitors who can offer us some feedback about the way we run things here.'

Erica saw Cleo stiffen, but she said only. 'That's what we've come to discuss, sir—Jon.'

'Well, pull up a chair, and let's hear all about it.' He pulled a notepad towards himself, picked up a pen, and gestured at the variety of chairs grouped in front of his desk. The five of them quickly chose seats and Erica ended up in the middle, with Toby on her left, Missy on *his* left, and Polly on her other side, with Cleo sitting a little further over, feet tucked up under herself.

'Missy was a client of the Centralia Fear Clinic,' Polly said. 'A good place. Excellent input. But they came here to warn us that things are going wrong.'

A frown crossed Jon's face. 'Not with Dale and Fiona, surely? They're two of the most stable people we have here.'

'Apparently not,' Cleo said.

'Go on,' Jon said. 'Tell me what happened.'

Erica laid the files on the desk in front of him. 'Three people died,' she said. 'Your doctors knew about it and they didn't do anything to stop it. They're putting people into more and more intense simulations just to harvest their fear instead of taking what's there already and letting it go at that. They drugged Toby and I and put us through one without our consent, and they were making Missy worse, not better.'

Jon's head drooped and he pulled the files towards him, opening each one and reading the first few lines before closing them again. 'I see,' he said sadly. 'It's a terrible thing when one of our people goes bad. Two at once is exponentially worse. I'll have them recalled at once and replaced.'

'I thought perhaps Nikola and Rupinder,' Polly said. 'If they're Rupinder at the moment.'

'I will contact them and find out. If you can bring Dale and Fiona to me as soon as possible, I'll contact Jojo and let her know that we need her assistance again.'

'No problem,' Polly said. She turned to Erica. 'You three know where Fiona and Dale are, don't you?'

'They're probably still at the Fear Clinic cleaning up after the fire,' Toby said. 'But we're out of this. This isn't our problem any more.' He still looked petulantly angry.

'All you need to do is bring them through the door and we'll take it from there,' Cleo said. 'I'll bring Harald out just for the occasion.'

Jon chuckled. 'He's your Viking warrior, isn't he?'

'More or less.' Cleo glanced sideways. 'They don't know about us yet.'

'Oh? Then you can explain when they come back from their retrieval mission.' Jon made it sound like an exciting game. 'Polly and Cleo, if you can return to the factory floor where these three came through, I'm sure they'll be back within minutes.' He turned his attention to the other three. 'Erica, Missy, Toby, I know that after what you've been through this will seem like an impossible task, but all you need to do is bring Dale and Fiona through the door to us.'

Erica stood up and took a deep breath. 'If you can show us how to get back to the clinic,' she said, 'I'm up for trying anything that will stop them.'

'Me too,' said Missy, looking as bravely determined as she could manage.

'Me three,' said Toby.

Jon smiled. 'Through that door,' he said, pointing to a door to his left in the wall behind his desk. Erica was getting thoroughly sick of doors with the unknown behind them, but something about Jon— some solid reassuring aura—made her feel that it was all right. She got up, went to the door, waited for the others to join her, and then opened it and stepped through.

CHAPTER THIRTEEN

When the world settled again they were back in the basement of the Fear Clinic, standing near the chair that Erica had strapped Doctor Morley into. He was gone now, and so were Doctor Chapman and the orderlies. The smoke was getting heavier, though, hazing the air. Time had passed, although whether it was the same amount of time that had passed in the ideas factory—a place that seemed to be outside time—or not, Erica wasn't sure.

'What in hell is going on here?' she choked, picking up a surgical mask out of a boxful on a bench and strapping it on. It helped a little, but her eyes were already stinging and watering.

'This is out of control,' Toby said, taking a mask for himself and passing Missy one. 'I didn't light anything on fire that should be doing this much damage.'

A piercing shriek resounded down the stairs from one of the upper rooms. It sounded vaguely familiar. Erica didn't wait to puzzle out who it was, though. She ran for the stairs, Toby and Missy at her heels, and pelted up them at top speed.

Doctor Chapman's office was deserted. So was the reception area. The front doors hung open and Erica heard the still-distant wail of a fire engine on its way up from Centralia.

The main corridor was full of smoke. She heard another shriek; this time it went up and up and then stopped before starting again, repeating the same cyclic pattern that she had heard before they'd broken into Doctor Chapman's office. It was coming from somewhere further down the corridor; one of the treatment rooms, it had to be. She went to the front door and, lifting her mask, drew a deep lungful of clean air.

Most of the clinic's patients and staff were out on the front lawn, the staff trying to count heads and usher people still further from the growing blaze.

The two head doctors weren't there.

'Where are they?' Toby was at her side and had realised the same thing.

'Making it worse. Covering it up.'

Missy's cheeks were a bright pink, which was both better and worse than the wan white she had been for a week. 'The evidence. Everything downstairs ... it'll be gone.'

Erica turned back to the smoky corridor. She could see the ominous red glow of flames coming through at least two doorways further down the hallway. She readjusted her mask and walked forward.

'Erica, are you crazy?' Toby asked in an almost conversational tone. 'You can't go in there, Erica ... Erica?'

Erica ignored him and plunged into the smoke.

It was easy enough to find her way by following the shrieking; though the smoke alarms were beeping incessantly and the fire alarm was filling the air with wails of its own, nothing else had that quality of pure, unadulterated terror. She had a moment to wonder if Polly and Cleo were monitoring that particular input, and then her fingers, trailing along the wall, found the open door.

A hand landed on her shoulder and she almost screamed, almost lost her lungful of good air, before realising that it was Toby. Missy was behind him, eyes wide above her mask.

Toby nodded into the smoke-filled darkness.

Erica nodded back and went in, hands outstretched, moving unerringly through the smoke. The thing about hospitals, no matter what sort of hospital they were, was that you were more or less guaranteed that the rooms would be virtually identical, and so she knew where to find the door of the treatment room. It was hanging open and the heat inside was approaching unbearable. She went in anyway, able to see now by the light of the flames. The doctors were in there. They were kneeling, they had someone pinned on the floor—a young man of her own age, with the flames reflected in his goggles, as if they needed any simulation for this to be terrifying. As she approached, he started shrieking again.

The doctors heard her too late. She didn't bother with the bone saw this time, instead kicking Doctor Morley as hard as she could in the temple. Doctor

Chapman tried to grab her and Toby brought the butt of his torch down on the back of her head.

'Missy,' Erica said, speaking through almost-closed lips. 'Get him out onto the steps. Yell for help. *Don't come back in.*' Missy took hold the boy's arm—he shrieked again—and pulled him to his feet, towing him towards the door so fast that he didn't have time to protest. His goggles hit the floor and then they were gone into the swirling smoke.

The ceiling was making alarming noises and Erica grabbed Doctor Chapman by the feet, dragging her out into the bedroom and through into the hallway. The fire was tasting the edge of the bedroom carpet now and liked it better than whatever slow-burning stuffing filled the treatment room's walls. Toby was close behind, bumping Doctor Morley along behind him like an unbalanced wheelbarrow.

They hurried back down the corridor through the thickening smoke and met Missy at the reception area.

'I told you not to come back in!'

'Shut up,' Missy said simply, taking one of Doctor Morley's legs to help Toby.

Two of the orderlies had come to get the boy but were already carrying him down the steps and didn't see what had happened to the doctors, fortunately enough, because Erica was having a hell of a time as it was and didn't really feel like letting it get any worse by needing to stop and fight off a couple of heavies in the middle of a burning building.

'Are you sure this is a good idea?' Toby yelled over the general racket of alarms.

'No! But it's the only one we've got!' Erica made for Doctor Chapman's office. Toby and Missy followed her without any further hesitation. They thumped down the stairs without any particular care for the doctors' heads (after all, the doctors hadn't paid much mind to theirs) and went through to the morgue.

Rose and Nathan and Linh were waiting there for them. Rose grinned savagely when she saw the doctors. 'We're coming with you,' she said.

'By all means,' Toby said. 'But let's *go*.'

Rose leapt through the doorway, still grinning, and Nathan and Linh followed her. Toby went through next, dragging Doctor Morley, and Erica paused for Missy to go.

'Go on,' Missy said. 'I'll shut the door.'

'Is that a good idea?' Erica asked.

'Don't know, but do you really want to come back through it? We'll get that guy Jon to beam us to somewhere else.'

Erica nodded and stepped into the blue haze.

Doctor Chapman's head thudded off the concrete floor; Erica dropped to one knee and checked to make sure that there wasn't any bleeding. There wasn't, but judging from the way the doctor groaned as Erica gently probed the back of her head with her fingers, there was going to be one hell of a bump for a while.

Polly joined her and helped her lift Doctor Chapman up properly. Cleo was nowhere to be seen. A solidly build blond man had thrown Doctor Morley over his shoulder and was briskly marching towards the rehabilitation room.

'Where's Cleo?'

'She's Harald at the moment,' Polly said. She caught the expression on Erica's face. 'Poor thing. This must be so strange for you. I'll explain as soon as I can. But for now we need to get these two around to rehab so that Jon can deal with them.'

Erica obediently helped her carry Doctor Chapman, who was beginning to stir, into the rehabilitation room. Harald had put Doctor Morley down on the couch, and while they were gone someone had brought in a wheeled bed, like a hospital gurney, so Erica had somewhere to put Doctor Chapman. After checking that they were both alive and well, Polly pressed a funny square patch like a Band-Aid onto each of their arms, and they both fell asleep. 'Transdermal sedative patch,' she said in response to Erica's curious look. 'Like a nicotine patch, except it sends them into la-la land for a while so we can talk to Jon.'

Jon was just saying goodbye to two other people when the horde descended upon his office—presumably Nikola and Rupinder, but they didn't hang around for introductions, instead going straight to the door behind the desk and through it.

'The clinic's on fire,' Toby said.

'Don't worry. They will come out elsewhere. I'd never send anyone knowingly into danger like that.' Jon nodded at the half-sized flat-screen computer monitor on the edge of his desk. 'I checked that before I sent you through, and before I sent them through. I always check to be certain that nobody is going to come out in mid-air, or in the middle of a riot, or in a burning building.' He folded his hands on his desk and looked at the group. 'Now, I think everyone had better sit down again so that we can all get to know each other.'

Erica was looking straight at Harald this time when his facial features flickered and rearranged into Cleo's. She was suddenly a few inches shorter, and her clothes changed as well, from jeans and a t-shirt back to her white lab coat-white polo shirt-black jeans ensemble.

'That's better,' she said. 'Harald's great for muscle, but he gets so *aggressive* sometimes.'

'Because *you* never do,' Polly remarked. She sat down and tugged Cleo onto her lap. 'Take a seat, everyone, and we can pow-wow.'

'I haven't done that since I was twelve,' Missy commented, but she sat down anyway. The ghosts looked uncertain about sitting down, but eventually Rose gave it a shot. Her eyes widened.

'I can touch the chair,' she said.

'You'll find that you're capable of touching everything for as long as you're here,' Jon said. 'The normal rules of reality don't exactly apply here.'

Rose got back up and threw her arms around Erica, who hugged her back. 'Thank you so much. I just knew you'd be able to avenge me—us.' She sat back down and Jon passed her a perfectly mundane looking box of Kleenex.

'I want to know what's going on with Polly and Cleo and Harald and people not being the same person all the time,' Toby said, sprawling in his seat—Erica caught him eyeing Polly and Cleo up. *Boys*, she thought.

'A place like this needs specialised staff, and it needs a lot of them,' Jon said. 'We don't have room to house all the staff we need if they were in different bodies. So we have special staff, who happen to be different people in one body.'

'Like dissociative identity disorder,' Erica said.

'Except that it's not a disorder here, that's more or less it,' Jon said. 'The difference is that when the frontrunner changes, their physical characteristics change as well—one of the other benefits of the laws of reality not quite applying. For multiples in your world, life is very often frustrating because people look at them and see the same face and body all the time, but the person looking out from behind the eyes is different.'

Erica considered this for a long moment. 'So do new staff have to give up their own body and time-share, or doesn't it work like that?'

'We rarely get new staff,' Jon said, 'and they're far more likely to arise from within an existing staff member than to come in from outside. People aren't supposed to know about this place ...' He sighed.

'I don't mind that you've come here, but you have to understand, this puts me in a bit of a quandary. If I send you back to your world, sooner or later you'll want to tell people about this place, especially if the police want to know where the doctors disappeared to and won't accept a medical conference as an excuse.'

'We won't tell,' Missy said.

'Not intentionally. But we can—look. If we remove your phobia, give Toby one good solid novel idea, and inspire someone to give Erica a great job, would you consent to having your memories of this place removed? You'd go back to your own world and wake up at home, and everyone would think you'd been there all along.' He nodded at Erica's dubious expression. 'Ideas don't just have to be for books. We can whip up the notion that you should be promoted to station manager PA and shoot it off.'

'Have you been doing background checks on us?' Erica asked bluntly.

'Of course,' Jon said, unruffled. 'We like to know about our visitors.'

'And what about us?' Rose asked. 'Where do we go from here?'

'You've got a number of options. You can't go back to your world, because you don't live there anymore.' Linh let out a sad sigh at this, and Jon leaned towards her, taking her hand in his. 'As you've noticed, though, you can touch things, so you can stay here if you wish.

That's option one. Option two is the machines. As you may have noticed, you were able to influence the virtual reality in your world even after you were dead because you could alter the electrical impulses. On a very basic level, that's what you are at the moment. So you can enter the machine and become part of someone's story. You can even specify what genre you'd like to enter, although of course plot twists can mean that a story that starts out as horror ends as fantasy, or vice versa.'

Rose shuddered. 'I don't think I would like to be in a horror novel, thank you,' she said flatly.

'Fair enough. The third—and final—option is the door.' Jon pointed to the door behind his desk with his free hand. 'I can specify where it leads, but I can also *not* specify any settings. If I do that, then you'll be sent on to wherever you were bound to go before you stayed in your world to seek vengeance for your death.'

'Where's that?' Linh asked, speaking for the first time. Her voice was shakily nervous, and Jon squeezed her hand comfortingly.

'Not even I know. It's different for everyone, I believe, but beyond that, I really can't say.'

'I think I'm going to stay here,' Rose said. 'At least this way I sort of have control over my own life, right?' She looked at Jon almost beseechingly, and Erica leaned over to put an arm around her.

'It's easy to learn the computers,' Polly said. 'There are always biscuits in the tin and fresh coffee in the machine, and you can even watch what's going on back home, if you wish.'

Rose shook her head. 'There's nothing for me there now.' She paused. 'I only have one question.'

'Yes?'

'Do I have to share a body with someone else?'

'Not at all,' Jon said. 'Not unless you decide you want to. I myself am single-natured, and I'm far from the only one.'

'I wanna go through the machine,' Nathan broke in; his voice was unsteady, breaking, reminding Erica that he'd only been young when he died, but his tone was adamant. 'I sure don't wanna work here forever, and what if there's *nothing* on the other side of that door? I reckon I deserve a second chance at living. God knows my first chance was garbage.'

Jon nodded. 'Then so you shall. Do you have a preference for where you would like to go?'

Nathan's brow furrowed. 'Dunno. I'll have to think about it.'

'Think away,' Jon said expansively. 'It's not as if you have a deadline to meet, after all.'

They all looked at Linh then. Linh was looking at the door, and had turned her hand over under Jon's so that she could grip his fingers tightly. Erica looked away, feeling as if she were intruding on a deeply personal, private moment.

'I think I would like to go through the door,' Linh said at last. 'I never felt—I never thought that I'd have to make this choice, but if I can't have the life I had, then ...' She got to her feet so quickly that the chair fell backwards; Nathan caught it one-handed and set it upright again. 'Thank you for offering me the choice.'

'The world would not be what it is without choices,' Jon said gravely. He pulled out a keyboard on a rolling shelf from beneath his desk and pressed a few keys. 'You may go whenever you are ready.'

Linh squeezed his hand one last time and then let go. They all watched her walk to the door, open it, and step through without looking back.

Later, none of them could agree upon what they had seen through the open door.

After that, Jon suggested that the rest of them go and give Rose and Nathan a tour of the place. 'It would probably be better for you to stay away from the rehabilitation room while Jojo works her magic,' he said as tactfully as possible.

When the door marked EXECUTIVE OFFICES closed behind them, Erica was secretly pleased that she didn't have to hang around. Rehabilitation could mean any number of things, but her mind kept flashing to a movie she'd watched when she was just a kid. It might not have been intended to be a horror flick—although quite a lot of scenes in it and in the movie it was a sequel to had kids crying out in fear— but the thing that had wigged her out when she'd watched it was the electroshock machine. The thought that psychiatric doctors had actually used such things on their patients had made her extremely uncomfortable, if not actually frightened.

'What're you thinking about, Erica?' Missy asked.

'*Return to Oz.*'

Missy nodded with a dubious expression on her face and went back to listening to Polly, who was repeating the explanation of the machines for Nathan and Rose's benefit.

Before much longer, Jon came out to where they were sitting in the tearoom. 'Jojo's stopped the problem in its tracks and is working to reverse it now,' he said. 'It'd be a shame to lose Dale and Fiona, so I'm glad it's working so well.' He sat down and took a milk arrowroot biscuit out of the tin.

'What would happen if—if the problem were irreversible?' Missy asked.

'They'd be reassigned,' Jon said. 'Probably to non-fiction. It's difficult to get carried away with non-fiction. Some people do manage it, but we'd send them to work on something nice and quiet.'

'How many non-fiction ideas ever need to be created?' Toby said somewhat scornfully.

'People need inspiration to be able to write master's theses or encyclopaedias just as much as they need inspiration to be able to write pulp horror,' Jon said severely. 'They need to have a direction in mind—a plot, almost—or just like a trunk novel, a non-fiction book can run out of steam and disappear into the nested folders on some would-be academic's PC.'

'Fair enough.' Toby crammed a whole Tim Tam into his mouth. Erica turned away in disgust and found herself looking straight into Jon's dark brown eyes. They were kind, but looked very tired.

'It's time for everyone to go where they're going,' he said.

'I'm staying here,' Rose said immediately.

'That's perfectly all right,' Jon said. 'But Nathan, you need to decide on your destination, and you three—' he indicated Erica, Missy, and Toby '—need to come back to my office. You'll be returned to the clinic, but outside rather than inside.'

'Gee, thanks,' Toby said, swallowing the last of his Tim Tam.

'Additionally, the other changes I mentioned will be implemented. Once you step through the door, you will forget this place. You will remember only that Missy came home because she was cured, and when your parents see that she is cured they will forgive your little upset. Toby, in a few days' time you'll start working on your novel. Erica, your job might be a bit harder to arrange, but rest assured it will happen soon.' Jon stood up. 'Let's go.'

Erica swallowed the last of her coffee, rinsed the mug in the sink, and walked as slowly as she could through the computer lab to the executive offices, looking all around, trying to fix every little detail in her mind. She carried the files that they had come to find, that would have burned with the clinic.

Polly and Rose stopped in the doorway to the executive offices to wave them off. Cleo was already bent over a computer keyboard with Nathan, intently discussing his options, but both of them called out their farewells as the trio followed Jon towards the personnel office.

'Take care of yourselves,' Polly said, giving each of them a quick, tight hug.

Rose hugged Erica for a long moment. 'Take those files straight to the police and tell them—oh, I don't care what you tell them, just make sure that nothing like this happens again.' Erica didn't know what she was going to tell the police, but an anonymous written statement wouldn't be a bad idea, rather than trying to talk her way through the story. Toby had all the writing skills; he would doubtless be able to whip something up.

'Wait!' Nathan called from the computer. He got up and hurried over to them. 'They buried my body in the garden,' he said. 'Linh's as well. Tell them that.'

'I will,' Erica promised. She grabbed a pen from one of the desks and made a note of it on the cover of Nathan's folder, knowing that she wouldn't remember of her own accord.

And then it was time to go through the door. Erica opened it with a feeling of trepidation, wondering whether Jon had really reset its destination after Linh had gone, or whether they would be stepping through into nothingness, but the smell of smoke reached her nose through the opened door and she knew that they were going home.

'Thank you,' she said to Jon.

Jon inclined his head. 'You're welcome.'

Erica pulled the door open wider and stepped through.

The fire hadn't yet reached the back garden of the clinic. It seemed that the sprinkler system wasn't malfunctioning after all, it had just taken a while to kick in. Erica felt the files under her t-shirt slipping as she scrambled up onto the wall, and tucked it in a little more tightly before jumping to the ground. The sound of fire engine sirens was getting closer, and the three of them piled into the car as quickly as possible, aware that the fire brigade would probably want to use the side road as an access point to the fire at the back of the clinic.

Getting back into the house once Toby had dropped them off was, in a way, the hardest part. They both had their house keys, but their parents' bedroom was at the head of the stairs and after all this time dealing with Missy's nightmares they were conditioned to waking up fairly quickly. The girls moved past as silently as they could manage, and made it into Erica's room without the light going on in their parents' room.

'What now?' Missy asked in a low voice.

'Now we get some sleep,' Erica said, sniffing her hair. 'Yuck—smoke.'

'Sleep sounds good,' Missy said.

'You want to crash in here?'

'Nah, I'll be fine.'

And she was. Erica heard her pad down the hallway, heard the soft thumps as her shoes hit the floor, followed shortly by her clothes, then the squeak of the bedsprings, and then a silence that lasted the rest of the night.

For her own part, Erica lay awake for another hour before her brain finally shut down for the night, thinking about what to do with the files, what to write in the letter she had decided should accompany the files, and debating what time to get up in the morning so that she could shampoo the smell of smoke out of her hair and get her clothes into the washing machine before her parents noticed.

They didn't notice anything.

Exactly what happened after she left the files and letter at Centralia Police Station, simply walking in and dropping it on the front counter when it was briefly unmanned, Erica was never a hundred percent certain. She knew that they ordered a digging operation at the Fear Clinic and uncovered two bodies—Toby was the reporter for that one—and that further investigations were being conducted. As far as she was aware though, Doctor Chapman and Doctor Morley had disappeared. She remembered seeing them at the clinic that night, but nobody ever seemed to find them again, and when a notice about the clinic's reopening (scheduled for the following July, when they hoped to have replaced all their expensive equipment and rebuilt the facility itself) appeared in the *Leader*, the doctors mentioned were two completely different faces with two completely different names. They seemed familiar, somehow—she supposed that they had probably already been on staff there and she'd seen them around the place.

With the Fear Clinic closed, even temporarily, and Missy sleeping peacefully through the night, it was hard for Erica to keep focussed on it all. She couldn't discuss it with her parents, and she didn't want to make Missy think about it at all, or Toby for that matter. She didn't know what to think about the ghosts. Sometimes it was hard not to think about it, especially at night, when every strange sound outside that turned out to be a possum or a scraping branch or an owl *might* have been a dead voice calling her for help.

Eventually, life moved on.

Epilogue

There were more leaves to skim off the surface of the pool every day. Erica finished the job, hung the net back on the hook on the side of the shed, and then realised that she didn't want to go swimming after all; the pool might be heated, but the air certainly wasn't. She walked once more around the pool, making sure the leaves were all gone; the filter was a pain to clean if it got clogged.

A piercing shriek cut through the air, and Erica was running before she quite realised it, yanking the back sliding door open and hurtling into the living room.

'Where's the fire?' Missy asked. She was sitting on the couch with Aaron, a crocheted blanket spread across both their laps, a big bowl of popcorn on the coffee table in front of them. Erica looked at the television screen and realised that the scream had only been the one that signalled the beginning of the movie *Scream*.

'Thought I heard the phone ring,' Erica mumbled. She filched a handful of popcorn and went upstairs. She only had another dozen books to move and they were all Point Horror and Fear Street; she didn't think she'd even bother putting them on the downstairs bookshelves, but would box them up and move them straight out to the shed. Clearing her bookshelves was a good idea, really. She'd had the same old books and movies for ages. It was time for a change.

She'd taken her *House on Haunted Hill* poster down too, when one silly night after having a drink with Toby she'd come home and been convinced that the hand was reaching out of the poster, trying to grab her. She was never going to drink raspberry vodka again after that little incident.

She considered calling Toby, but he was writing at light speed these days; some book idea he'd come up with called *The Lust Gatherers*. It most definitely had nothing to do with his job. Although he was sitting pretty there, with a pay rise after his series of reports on the Fear Clinic deaths. The page or two she'd caught a glimpse of once before he closed the window was far too salacious to be any sort of current affairs report for the *Lilywood Leader*—the *Penthouse Forum*, maybe.

That left washing the dinner dishes—well, putting them in the dishwasher—or having another go at the computer game Toby had lent her. She chose the game—it had become surprisingly addictive, and hacking away at trolls and endless quantities of kobolds was an excellent source of stress relief. She was enjoying her new job as station manager PA, but it was more demanding than being a receptionist. The pay made up for it, though—as she'd started in December, when one of the other two PAs had announced that she was going on a Christmas break and not coming back, she'd been able to pay off the horrendous amount of Christmas gifts she'd put on her credit card.

After what seemed like five minutes on the computer she checked the time and was startled to see that it was ten o'clock. She was going to have to go to bed if she wanted to get enough sleep before work the next day.

She'd been waking up every so often during the night with vaguely remembered dreams still floating unattached to anything in particular in her mind. There was rarely more to these memories than darkness and the sound of running water. Nothing, really. And she usually got back to sleep within ten or fifteen minutes.

The nightlight she'd put in in early February helped—the bathroom light had blown, and they hadn't had a spare fluoro tube, and though she'd initially only borrowed the nightlight from Missy until the bathroom light was replaced a week later, she'd held onto it just in case it was the socket that was faulty and the new fluoro tube blew as well. She just didn't want to trip over anything in the dark. She only turned it on when she needed to get up, and sometimes if she'd woken up in the night with the shadows watching her.

She didn't really like using it. Not with the eerie clown face, eyes watching her knowingly, deeper and darker than the shadows.

She said goodnight to her parents and to Missy, changed into her pyjamas, and crawled into bed. If she were lucky, she'd fall asleep while they were still up, before the house went completely silent except for the leaky tap in the bathroom that her father kept promising to have fixed but hadn't quite done anything about yet.

She didn't like lying there thinking about the waste of water, that was all. It was quite a brisk drip. Thinking that it might get faster still bothered her. She wasn't *afraid*, just environmentally conscious.

The orange standby light on her computer monitor looked a bit like a waiting eye in the darkness. Erica got up, turned the monitor off entirely, and then went back to bed.

Sleep was a long time in coming.

ABOUT THE AUTHOR

Lauren E. Mitchell lives in Melbourne, Australia with their husband and assorted cats. When they aren't writing they may be working, reading, or crying over whatever just happened in the latest episode of whichever web series currently holds their attention. They are pretty sure their pile of books to be read is going to eat them. If you want to contact them before their inevitable death by unread books, here are some ways you can do that:

Facebook:
http://www.facebook.com/laurenmitchellwrites

Twitter:
http://twitter.com/LEBMitchell